ARTIFICIAL LORDS

BOOK ONE
DIVISION

ADAM NORWOOD

Print ISBN: 978-1-09831-061-5

eBook ISBN: 978-1-09831-062-2

CONTENTS

ELI

Eli Ritchie awakened April 16, 2076, yet again eager to continue his quest for success as a human musician. He knew it was an uphill battle. He was 23, a recent music school graduate from Berkley, after rejecting his famous father's path into science. It would seem Eli was made to be a musician: He could play many instruments, was blessed with an outstanding voice — and he could compose. Despite all that, he had a difficult time finding work. His competitors were the musicians of yesteryear; new sounds and ideas had difficulty gaining traction. Eli never relented, though. He rose every day to make his own name and perfect his craft.

Tomorrow, he'd start a six-week gig at an out-of-the-way venue called Real Singers in a left-behind section of Oakland. Eli hadn't performed publicly for two months, so he was relieved to have secured the contract, though the pay was quite low. He was determined to generate interest in human musicians again, especially himself. Eli had rejected the new trend of routinely replacing human body parts, such as knees and hips, at a young age. He figured at some point he would use gene therapy to extend his lifespan — he wasn't a fool, after all — but he was determined to truly be himself for as long as he could.

Eli started his day with a 10-mile run through the neighborhoods of San Francisco. He'd start from his home near Fisherman's Wharf, then head southwest toward the Pacific Ocean and finally loop back home. Technology was moving at such a blistering pace these days that the scenery he witnessed along the route would change almost daily. Often, he would pass the familiar cast of characters, Frank Sinatra, Marilyn Monroe, or perhaps Ernest Hemmingway. Today, a couple miles into his run, he passed Elvis walking the family dog. Seeing these replicas, as they were called, of long-deceased icons was not unusual, but he also passed a rapper and an athlete who had achieved fame during Eli's early childhood. Apparently, the real celebrities had sold their likenesses while still alive, a practice rapidly becoming commonplace, thanks to the high royalties they garnered. As he turned north again, he knew he might run into some famous 20th Century musicians near the park. It seemed that Jerry Garcia had never fallen out of favor in San Francisco, and you could often see a replica of the famous Grateful Dead band leader playing his guitar in Golden Gate Park while a group of folks gathered to watch. On this morning, though, Jerry was alone, probably just fetching coffee for his family. The one thing Eli knew as he jogged by these beings is that they were almost all HARE Corporation models, creations of the company his father built.

As Eli ran past the replicas, he was reminded of the NASA mission launched three years earlier to reach the Proxima solar system. It held a planet that scientists had discovered evidence of having life — one that was close enough that humans could reasonably travel there. The targeted planet was named Perth by using a combination of the solar system Proxima and its likeness to Earth. Eli wondered what might happen when the spaceship arrived. If there was intelligent life, what would the reaction be to the beings NASA decided to send? They had carefully selected humanoid replicas of such iconic figures as Princess Diana, Martin Luther King and Gandhi to greet the Perthians. It was incredibly exciting to think humans might be able to communicate with other intelligent beings in the near future, but Eli wondered what would happen if the other cultures had developed in the same way as humans? Would our human imposters end up meeting fake aliens? Is that even a real encounter? What was real anymore, Eli wondered.

Halfway into his run, Eli stopped for coffee at a place called Natalie's Golden Brew. The proprietor, of course, had a Hollywood resume. Natalie Wood appeared behind the counter.

Eli just couldn't get excited about greeting replicas, no matter how impressive their reproduction. He never looked directly at them, either, maybe a quick glance before he turned his head away.

"Good morning, Eli, welcome back to Natalie's!" she said. Replicas never forgot your name, because they were built with a facial recognition feature. That's why the first time you'd meet a replica like Natalie, she would always ask for your name.

"Thanks, can I have the Mariacino?" The beverage had the "Maria" prefix added to highlight Natalie Wood's character in West Side Story. Why can't I just order a damn cappuccino, Eli thought to himself? Down the street at Capone's, it's called the Al-Capocino. How many ways can you bastardize the name of drink?

"Coming right up," Natalie said. Of course, she didn't do anything herself. The brew automatically appeared on the counter. The interaction with the fake Natalie Wood was just a wasted exercise, in Eli's opinion. These days there was no need for a server to produce a cappuccino — or anything else you ordered, for that matter. Fully automated restaurants with voice-based ordering had been perfected many years ago, but restaurateurs noticed that without the human interaction, people became less interested in going out. Restaurants soon hired humans, but later replaced them with humanoids and, later, replicas when that more advanced iteration of human replacements became available. People were fearful of the humanoids at first, thanks to all the TV shows and films that predicted humanoids' eventual conquest of humanity. Before too long, though, humanoids became commonplace, especially here in Harmony. So far, humanoids were not the danger people had feared. Eli didn't share that fear, as his father had told him long ago that humanoids were built without survival instincts, consciousness and feelings. It was forbidden by U.S. law, and no one had dared to open that Pandora's Box. Humanoids had only the qualities given to them by their human developers. The real danger was always how humanity had evolved — and what human traits such as competition and greed would lead them to do with robots and humanoids. Eli grabbed his coffee and sat down. He saw a man staring at him, and Eli turned his head in that direction.

"Hey, stranger," he said. "I thought that was you, Eli. It's been quite a long time. How's it going?" Eli immediately recognized the man who presented him a warm smile that Eli returned.

"Ramsey, how are you?" Eli replied in the much more enthusiastic manner he reserved for other humans, at least ones he liked. He headed toward Ramsey's table.

"I'm fine, Eli, just fine. I've kind of settled into a different life these days." Ramsey was a longtime associate of Eli's father and had left the company seven years earlier.

"Oh yeah? I have no idea what you do now. Obviously, we haven't seen each other in years. I don't know how you even recognized me."

"Ah, that wasn't difficult; you look the same. I spend my time on the other side now. I just find it more tolerable. I feel like it's just a big theme park over here. Everything is perfect, all the time, except of course it's not. At some point I just had to get out. Besides visiting my company, which is just over the border in Jackson, Wyoming, I spend at most a couple of weeks a year on this side. Only because I need to."

"Really, you live in Hope? I've not been there; what's it like? I don't hear many good things. Isn't it dangerous?"

"It can be, but that's something I'm trying to help change. Hey, Eli, I actually have to go. Tell you what: Come over to my house in Hope and visit sometime. You'll find out exactly what it's like. I promise you'll be safe." Ramsey handed Eli an old-fashioned business card. Such cards had come back in vogue to combat identity thieves — no one would have your information other than those you personally gave it to.

"Good seeing you, Eli."

"You too, Ramsey. You, too." Eli uttered the phrase a second time as if to reinforce that their meeting had meant something to him. As Eli finished his run, he could not stop thinking about Ramsey and the other side.

IAN RAMSEY

Ramsey, as everyone called him, lived in Hope near a western border of Harmony in a town called Red Lodge, Montana. It was near the Beartooth Highway and the Laramie Valley in Yellowstone. Two days after his trip to San Francisco, and his chance meeting with Eli, Ramsey was back in the place he loved most. Unlike virtually all of the inhabitants of Hope, Ramsey was wealthy and lived there of his own volition. He brought his vast resources across the border to live freely in a world that was much less controlled and scripted. He could never accept his every action being tracked and recorded as if his whole existence were a motion picture. Ramsey gladly traded predictable and safe for something that offered excitement, and more importantly, a purpose.

Ramsey's home was a beautiful fortress built on Rock Creek at the base of the Beartooth Mountains. He had loved the outdoors ever since he could remember, and being on the border of Yellowstone was a perfect location for him much of the year. The winters were a bit too frigid and restricted his travel so he usually would head south by late October to his other dwelling in extreme Southeast Colorado near Durango. Both locations were close enough to his manufacturing plant in Jackson Hole for him to visit in person if he needed to. Because the journey from Durango was quite a haul, he didn't visit the plant very often that time of year. This place in Red Lodge was his favorite, though. He could sit on a boulder at the edge of the creek, which meandered throughout his property, and ponder whatever encompassed his mind. From there he could look up at his vast wooden porch, where he'd likely spend his evenings. They would be filled with virtual meetings and discussions, which again reminded him of his purpose. The daytime respite on the creek gave him the peace he needed to clear his mind and refocus on the task at hand. The current task was quite a daunting one, indeed.

Ramsey had lived alone for almost two decades after his wife divorced him, saying he was too married to his work. That foreshadowed of things to come, as his only companions now were the creations of his work product. They and the residence he had built for them were what gave him comfort now. Though Ramsey did maintain relationships with several of his humanoids, he didn't seem to be the type who could design the perfect one and try to develop a single monogamous relationship with her alone. Maybe it was because he was the designer and he knew what was really inside. It probably made it impossible to think of them as human, let alone a girlfriend or spouse.

The inside of this home was a lesson in American history. Each room represented a different period of America's past, some sections going back to Native American times. The great room was the centerpiece and where Ramsey spent most of his time. It was shaped in a giant oval with an adjacent porch spanning the width of the room; the divider between them was all glass, ensuring an unspoiled view of the creek. This room represented 19th Century America broken down into 10 sections, each representing a particular decade. Visitors were greeted by a map of Lewis and Clark's expedition and figurines portraying the legendary duel between Hamilton and Burr. The last section just inside the door displayed a brilliantly colored model of the 1853 New York City World's Fair and a "Remember the Maine" banner.

From there, guests would see doorways to the other sections of the enormous home. One door led to a great library filled from floor to ceiling with books; another was the entrance to a room that paid homage to the Colonial period of America. A beautiful massive wooden stairway in the center of the room led to the eight-bedroom second floor, each splendidly adorned with relics from the 20th Century. Nowhere in the home could you find anything from the 21st Century, a clear statement from Ramsey. It was obvious to anyone with whom he spoke with that he felt this is where it all went wrong. His home made it clear to visitors Ramsey longed to be in a time and place he'd never see.

Ramsey also still owned the humanoid and robotics company he founded after splitting with Jack Ritchie. It was called simply called I Ramsey Inc. He didn't have a fancy marketing name or advertising strategy like HARE. He'd rely on his reputation to carry the new business. After all, he was the most talented and key engineer at HARE, while Jack had been more of the marketing genius. Jack was still a scientist in title and degree, but was never the real brains behind the technology, Ramsey felt. Jack ended up taking credit for many of Ramsey's innovations, which was a main reason for their split. Despite his aversion for Harmony, he set up his business there. He never could have secured some of his current contracts, especially government ones, if the plant were here in Hope. He rarely went there in person, anyway. He simply used virtual reality from his home offices in Red Lodge or Durango to make an appearance — via a robot that he'd direct to any part of the factory. The few human employees who worked there were accustomed to seeing Ramsey pictured within the robot.

The factory also contained some functional robots that did many of the jobs requiring physical labor; an extensive humanoid division was created by Ramsey, too. The one thing he didn't do was humanoid replicas. HARE had cornered the market there, so he left it to them. His humanoids were custom designed to be used as companions or whatever else you wanted. He also supplied the government with some of their fighting drones, which now comprised more than 90 percent of the nation's military. For that reason, Ramsey had to be *extremely* careful; his reputation was impeccable and allowed him to operate without suspicion. That he lived in Hope would normally raise questions, but he was thought of as a reclusive genius who loved the seclusion and beauty of the outdoors. He worked extremely hard to keep this reputation intact. Beneath that façade, though, he was without question the most important champion for the people of Hope.

THE RITCHIE FAMILY

On the same day Ramsey had arrived back home in Red Lodge, Eli decided to spend the evening at his parents' home. He would be working every night for a while, and they wouldn't get the chance again anytime soon. After having dinner and some drinks, they sat down for the usual live entertainment. When the performer was ready, he bowed his head slowly, looking at the floor for several seconds.

"I started writing this song in 1977. I struggled with finishing it for a couple of years and even changed the title a few times. I initially called it 'Emotional Wreck,' which tells you a lot," John Lennon said with a laugh. "It was such a personal song for me, which was why it was so difficult. I had gotten tired of answering the same questions repeatedly about why I left music, and this was my answer. It's one of my all-time favorites including all the music I did with the Beatles."

The sweet sound of his guitar rang out with the chords to "*Watching the Wheels.*" Eli's dad Jack, mother Melinda and Eli sang along. They loved John, and of course, that's why they picked him as their personal replica. When Eli was a young boy, Beatles music played throughout the house. John brought them back to the time of being a young family. It was a warm feeling with deep meaning to all of them. John had also been created with a personality culled from his interviews, which allowed the Ritchies to stay up late at night and listen to John's ideas. They were now 100 years old, but still fascinating to Jack and family. Many still resonated, as the problems that existed during John's time had never been solved. Designers intentionally omitted negative behaviors, which John had admitted to having in his younger years, from their replicas. So, in many ways, the faux Lennon was a more perfect version. John finished the song and soon disappeared into a doorway down the hall while the Ritchies went upstairs to retire for the night.

Jack Ritchie spent most of his time at The Ritchie School for Humanoid Studies, a college named after him due to his generous financial endowment. He had been a humanoid pioneer all his life, and his dream to create a humanoid version of John Lennon had come true a few years earlier. Having John here to entertain his family never got old. Even though Jack was one of the wealthiest people in America, he owned only one humanoid. His home, though, was completely automated. Jack did have thoughts of what could be possible with all types of humanoids around, but he and his wife Melinda resisted. They were keenly aware that it was a path fraught with danger. They had each personally witnessed sexual affairs taking place between humans and humanoids. They didn't need more personalities or competing interests, so they lived by their own rules. Robots, technology, automation — yes. Humanoids beside John in the house — definitely no.

Jack was born in northern New Jersey in 2018, the son of Samuel Ritchie, an executive at a hip replacement company in the area. Human replacement parts, and the procedures to install them, were improving in leaps and bounds. Samuel had urged Jack to focus on robotics and biology. He knew the future would be filled with robots and humanoids that would take most of the jobs. Due to his father's foresight and wealth, Jack made his fortune in being at the right place at the right time. His father's guidance on getting degrees in both fields had paid off handsomely. His timing couldn't have been better, either, as the first practical application of quantum computing, the use of tiny particles such as electrons and protons to make computer processors millions of times faster, had been created shortly after Jack's birth. This was a game-changing technology whose first applications were in cloud-based business systems, but its first practical consumer use was in robotics. The enormous potential of this technology would lead to advanced humanoid creation. After graduating and working for a leading Japanese robotics firm, Jack dipped into a trust set up by his father to establish his company — Humanoids, Automation and Robotics Engineering, or the HARE Corp. — which ended up being the dominant company in the industry. HARE first focused on robotics and evolved to humanoids and finally humanoid replicas. Many players emerged in the field, but it was the marketing that set Jack's company apart. HARE featured a wise-cracking rabbit. At first, the similarities to the Looney Tunes' Bugs Bunny were obvious and caused Jack some trademark issues. So, HARE changed the rabbit's appearance, name and voice, but not his sharp wit. Bugsy Rabbit, as they called him, became a sensation. What captured people's imaginations almost 150 years earlier, had once again grabbed a new generation, catapulting HARE to become one of the largest companies in the world. The mass production of robots and humanoids, and the more specialized humanoid replicas, had created the greatest shift in world history.

Jack and Melinda spent most of their time at their home overlooking San Francisco Bay. They had other places along the beach in Southern California and Hawaii. They also owned the most lavish residence in Vail, as well as property in other countries. All were kept in perfect working order by robots, the precursors to humanoids and Jack's replicas. The San Francisco residence included a glass wall on the Bay side that operated on voice commands. It was quite a sight. Jack and his family would spend time in the custom mahogany banquette that faced the glass wall and listen to John, enjoyed meals or whatever else happened to be going on. The family hadn't been gathering as much since Eli had reached adulthood. Jack was secretly happy Eli still lived with them, even though outwardly Melinda and Jack often reminded Eli it was time to move out and build his own life. His lack of willingness to establish himself was certainly not a question of affordability. Eli, and his heirs for generations, would never need to worry about money.

Retired from HARE for a few years, Jack now spent most of his time at the college named after him. It allowed him to keep a close connection to the field he had helped pioneer. It was a connection he needed. After all, he had built his life around this technology, and even he didn't know where it was going. He didn't believe anyone really did. The college's ambitions lately had changed though based on what everyone really wanted them to focus on, human life extension. Their original charter had centered on how humans would coexist with humanoids, but the school was now caught up in the race to improve the human condition and provide them with longer lives. All funding lately was directed toward that goal. Jack's own purpose had shifted in that direction as well. He was not getting any younger, and replacement parts and other advances became more important to him every year.

HOPE

Asking humans to coexist with their creations had a downside: It separated those who owned robots and humanoids, benefitting from their productivity, and those who did not. Eventually, it led to a physical separation. Jack Ritchie had played a major role in making this happen, and at times he felt guilty about it. Throughout history, the wealthy needed the working class to perform the jobs they didn't want, such as caring for other humans as domestic workers, or keeping their communities functioning as police officers, firefighters and construction workers. With humanoids and robots created specifically to be superior at these tasks, millions of workers were displaced every year. They had little chance of returning to work as there was no task they were better at than what software automation, robots or humanoids could achieve. Now, with the more specialized humanoid replicas, even performers like Eli Ritchie were threatened. More than half the population of the U.S. was part of a new, seemingly permanent, underclass. Conflicts arose, and the rich and the poor were given separate zones in which to live. The federal government created the Hope Zone and the Harmony Zone. Hope was more or less a welfare state, designed for those not working who needed monthly Government Approved Payments to survive. GAP had become a reality about 10 years earlier, intended for those people displaced from the workforce by the same technological advances which ultimately led to the creation of the zones. Intended for people who were jobless and had little net worth, qualification was made by measuring existing wealth. It quickly became clear that the monthly

GAP payment was not enough to survive. People on GAP, who were rather contemptuously called Gappers by others, demanded the government do something about it. Eventually, they got their wish, but with a catch. People would be required to move to Hope to collect their income. The rich simply didn't want the Gappers around anymore and found a convenient way to get them to leave.

The zones were separated by a virtual wall controlled by huge power stations located within the Harmony zone. This made it quite easy to adjust borders, which was done frequently in the beginning to correct many initial errors like separating individual land parcels. The virtual wall visually resembled the Great Wall of China, but more than double the height. The 50-foot-tall virtual wall came at the insistence of the residents of Harmony, eventually referred to as *Harmonians*, to provide them better security and privacy.

Many soon referred to areas of Hope as "The Badlands." Beside including the actual Badlands of South Dakota, which could produce absolutely nothing, it also comprised many other undesirable locations either bereft of water or severely polluted. Of course, Harmonians were loath to give up such exquisite Wyoming landmarks as Yellowstone and the beauty of Jackson Hole, so they happily acquiesced the barren highland desert areas of that same state. This was the typical method used to divide the two zones. Hope included mostly poor cities. Larger cities with wealthy downtowns became part of Harmony, and anyone who didn't *belong* there quickly relocated to Hope to receive their incentive. Many homeless, who couldn't decide for themselves, were simply moved to the Hope side of the wall by the federal government. Such decisions were the product of Harmonian influence and reflected where they wanted to vacation and already owned property. Harmony mainly comprised the East and West coasts, but also included a big part of Texas. Gappers who would be forced from Harmony had little power to dispute border claims. Harmonians had purchased most of the land there, anyway. They saw the wall as a fence put around their privately owned paradise. Harmony and Hope were similarly positive labels for areas that couldn't be more dissimilar. Nearing her 300th birthday, America hadn't been as divided since the Civil War. Of course, the Ritchies lived in Harmony and most of the time were oblivious to the hardships of the people in Hope.

There were some notable exceptions of high-quality land within Hope that made it survivable. Those included the fertile soils of Nebraska and Kansas, which produced most of the food. Hope also included many areas of the Old West, and ironically, the place had regressed to those times in many ways. Not that it was again alive with horses, stagecoaches and rail cars; instead, the new Old West borrowed from the dangerous and lawless part — with one notable exception: the weapons were much more advanced and lethal. There were also people very skilled and intent on using them. This only fed the notion among Harmonians that Gappers were dangerous.

With creation of the two zones was a new, sublevel of government: Governors and their minions represented each of the new zones. The rich had already wielded enormous power over the federal government, and the Harmonians leveraged this into even greater influence that bordered on direct control. Harmonians had insisted on two major conditions if they were going to fund the increase in GAP. First, residents of Hope could travel to Harmony only with a passport, effectively establishing two classes of citizenship. Also, in exchange for the GAP being tripled, federal elections were dramatically overhauled. The message, "Three times the payment, one third the vote," was constantly broadcast on all media channels during the negotiations. Gappers were so focused on improving their own financial situation that they allowed this hard stance to be adopted without compromise. With a Harmonian's vote counting three times as much as ballots cast by Hope residents, this ensured that all presidential candidates would favor Harmonian policies almost exclusively in elections, save for the meaningless givebacks to Gappers, which were always overstated. No one did the math except for the future Harmonians, but now the math was clear: Gappers were destined for a life of constant regression and exploitation.

Governors elected by the residents of each zone theoretically were given equal power. In actuality, though, their powers were vastly different. Harmony Governor Paul Bento had more say in affairs than even the President of the United States. The autonomy of U.S. presidency and federal government had continued to weaken over many decades due to the increasing influence of the rich. That influence was now concentrated within Harmony and manifested itself in this new powerful Harmonian governor position. Caiden Calloway, the Hope governor, constantly witnessed legislation favoring Harmonians breeze through the House and Senate and signed into law by President Emma Johansson. With that structure, Hope was set up to fail from the start. Although sold with slogans such as "A place to start again" and the "Land of opportunity" to represent America's past, Hope was becoming more chaotic and violent by the day. Western style gunslingers were reborn and travelled from city to city injecting fear into the residents. Businesses failed at an unimaginable rate in border towns adjacent to Harmony. As people crowded into these urban areas, a sense of restlessness overcame the population, suppressed only by their daily dependence on the mood-altering drug of choice or escaping the madness in some computer-generated virtual reality world.

HARMONY

The wealthiest of Harmonians were mostly technology founders and their heirs such as the Ritchie family. It also included the sons, daughters, and grandchildren of executives of former prominent American industries such as finance and energy. Of course, decedents of past Hollywood royalty had their place as well, as did the heirs of the former great American music industry. Because the wealthiest of the wealthy lived in the Bay Area, San Francisco was selected as the Harmony capital. No small irony that the former bastion of liberal politics had become the center of wealth preservation in present day America. The founders of great technology companies had started their firms with the greatest intentions for humanity, particularly when it became clear that their own personal wealth and their heirs for generations would never be in doubt. Those intentions faded however among the splintered benefactors who never knew what it took to build or create anything. Harmonians instead became very good at protecting their own wealth and place within the elite. The used genetic modifications on their offspring to create a superior lineage and technology to enhance their own existence. They spent vast amounts of their wealth on funding human life extension projects like the one Jack Ritchie was involved with to make sure they were the ones who received the first working applications. Some even went into politics to ensure the message from their families were heard and favored over others. Paul Bento was one of those people.

Paul's father Peter had created one of the two most successful software companies the world had ever seen, and had even become the world's first trillionaire. Peter had championed many philanthropic initiatives in his later years, and was even the founder of a new American political party, American Intelligence, whose power and ideas actually led to the initial GAP payment. Peter had also embraced the Humanism movement — a new political theory on how humans should govern themselves in a world that contained superior beings, humanoids, born of humanity's own creation. It was supposed to supplant all other "isms" such as communism, socialism, and capitalism, deeming them irrelevant in this new paradigm. Their efforts failed, however, as their intentions to balance income and wealth never resulted in action, especially within the poorest areas of America. Their reliance on change via government channels ultimately disappointed, and their personal intentions to eventually distribute their wealth outside of their own families never happened for the most part. Even in cases where large inheritances were distributed it was mostly squandered by ineffective organizations and charities.

JOE AND EMILY

The governments of Hope and Harmony relied on virtual Artificial Intelligence personalities for their communication to the people, because these 'beings' were far superior to any human at performing this task. Unlike humanoid replicas these personalities never took on a physical form, but their faces could be seen virtually everywhere so they were as well-known as any human. Governor Caiden Calloway of Hope communicated his political positions using the Hope artificial being simply known as Joe. The name had been selected to represent everyman, an everyday Joe or Joe Six-pack. Joe also had a soothing voice which could be heard and seen by the public, especially in Hope, pretty much every day. Joe was rather convincing too because of his extreme intelligence and ability to simplify even the most complex topics to a message people could understand. Joe would immediately comment on current events, having the ability to form opinions quickly in order to lobby for the residents of Hope.

Just like Joe in Hope, Harmonians had a name for their Artificial Intelligence character: Emily. She also was convincing and pleasant to listen to as she presented her "fact-based" opinions. Amazingly, both Joe and Emily used the same 'facts' to come up with entirely different positions and outcomes. Both Joe and Emily were actually just virtual faces of giant supercomputers housed in each of the capital cities of the zones. Emily in San Francisco and Joe in Nashville. The enormous data centers where they were housed were well always well-guarded and secured. Both supercomputers were too important to be shut down or hacked in any way as they also managed many other services such as coordinating the robotic workers who maintained society.

Messages from the AI personalities Joe and Emily would be seen everywhere in text communications, video feeds, and other delivery channels within their zone. Virtual billboards within Hope and Harmony also lit up with the faces of Joe and Emily when they had something to communicate. The most striking example was when the enormous virtual wall itself was used as a giant billboard with Joe and Emily broadcasting opposing messages on each side, often at precisely the same moment. The communication style of using direct social media channels to communicate with potential voters mimicked what had become of human politicians more than 60 years earlier. At that time, however, the tone was often inflammatory and content at times bereft of facts. Joe and Emily always leveraged facts and were programmed to never offend.

LUCAS, SKY, AND LEXI

On the outskirts of Hope's urban areas, criminals roamed among the abandoned decay. Robotic police patrols entered these locations only on specific missions to incarcerate fugitives who had disrupted the more civilized neighborhoods. One such most wanted was 4-foot 7-inch tall Tim Lucas. He would appear out of nowhere and then quickly fade into the shadows, but before doing so often leaving a pile of corpses behind. The crimes he committed, like the 2074 killing of two of his rivals in a gunfight, were intentionally never directed towards the innocent. There were instances of collateral damage however, like a young woman killed by stray bullets in the same battle. There were others like him in Hope, but he was the most notorious and deadly. Though operating throughout most of his life as a vicious thug, few were aware he also possessed a deep intelligence which helped him elude capture for years.

Lucas was never seen in public without his cowboy hat and his gun belt with a pistol donned on each side. He was fan of the Old West and the western movies of the 20th Century and acted the part. He would often imagine himself as one of those western bandits and had even developed his own imposing glare, which he often revealed right before a real act of violence. Lucas had met the replica of one of these long-gone western actors when he travelled to Harmony a few years back; now he had incorporated some of the actor's mannerisms, including the glare. The replica he impersonated was one of the most highly reviewed replicas created so far and his meeting had clearly made a mark on Lucas. The detail in his appearance and his voice were extraordinary. Of course, people knew the original actor only from his films, making it easy to copy those characteristics and match people's expectations of him. Meeting the humanoid version made Lucas feel even more like him or, more accurately, his most famous character. He knew he would never have his height or looks, but he did have his fearlessness and the swift draw to back it up. And he did have a name. People referred to him simply as Lucas.

Lucas also had friends in high places allowing him to continue to operate without being captured. He spent most of his time in the Southwest from West Texas through Nevada. He didn't have a permanent residence, but instead roamed among several places where his acquaintances lived. They actually were homes he owned, but none were in his name. This allowed him to travel freely among these different locations without worrying about being turned away. It was a great bargain for the folks who lived in these safe houses, which ensured they would never betray Lucas. They often wondered how Lucas got all of his money as it seemed excessive for someone who lived his life as a criminal. Could he possibly have gotten rich from stealing? It was very difficult to get wealthy from thievery these days as the world had shifted to digital currencies. There seemed to be an endless supply of money around Lucas, though, so it was always fun when he was in town as he would pay the bill. Plus, in the last couple of years he was always accompanied by two very interesting female companions.

Like Lucas, the women wore cowboy hats and also donned long leather western boots. The three of them together looked like an old time western photo you would get of your family at a tourist site. Lucas had been seen a great deal less in public once he began his relationship with the two ladies, named Sky and Lexi. As a result, he also had fewer criminal incidents, dropping him down a few spots from the top of most wanted lists; however, he would never drop very far due to the violent nature of his previous crimes. His new companions led to his lessened interest in making trouble. They were Lucas' friends, soldiers and lovers — created to be just that by Lucas' close friend, Ian Ramsey. For that, Ramsey would always have Lucas' loyalty. Moreover, his two beautiful companions were easily capable of getting them out of any difficult situation. In many cases, Sky and Lexi were more capable than Lucas. He was the boss, though, as he was still the only one who had any human parts, and the humans still ruled. Lucas thought that would likely change in the coming decades. That didn't bother him all that much. He would often remind himself how much he hated most humans, anyway.

Lucas and his humanoid companions were traveling within Hope once again on a mid-April day in 2076. They had been summoned to a meeting with Ramsey and were on their way there now in their custom Air Enabled Vehicle (AEV), the official term for a flying car. Their model, a 2074 BlueJay, was communicated with just like a human using the built-in Artificial Intelligence-based personality named Jay. Lucas asked Jay to touch down in Leadville, Colorado, a town of 10,000 feet in elevation. They were close enough to reach Ramsey tonight but were not scheduled to meet until the morning. They would camp here tonight by the headwaters of the Arkansas River. The Harmony border near Vail was very close, so they would need to keep a careful watch on things. Although Lucas was extremely careful to make sure there was no way for him to be tracked, it was a constant battle. Being free meant giving up many things, and ironically it really meant you weren't free at all. There were no good choices for Lucas in this world, but this life was the only one he could accept.

Lucas, looking forward to seeing Ramsey, knew something big was up. Lucas could never use any standard technology to communicate if he wanted avoid capture, and worse, be linked to Ramsey. They only spoke in person, but they had creative means for Ramsey to summon Lucas. This was one of those times.

Lucas awoke by 6 a.m., while Sky and Lexi had their hydrogen-based fuel cells refilled from Jay, who used the same fuel. A few minutes each from the BlueJay was all it took for them to be completely recharged and able to stay on watch throughout the night.

The BlueJay had been modified by Ramsey and Lucas specifically to hide from tracking and robotic police. The modifications were extremely useful and effective, and there was no way they could survive without them.

"Good morning, my beauties," Lucas said as he rose from the temporary bubble shelter where he slept. "How was it out here? Anything flying around?" Lexi and Sky both shook their heads.

What they were watching out for were the solo-flying robotic police. These units were a normal part of everyday life in metropolitan areas and even small towns everywhere. In rural areas it was rare to see one buzzing by, and if you did, they were typically there for a specific purpose or mission. There were also crafts larger than a BlueJay that housed several robotic police for more difficult missions. They didn't expect to see anything like that out here.

"Well, we should be going soon," Lucas said, "but before we do how about a little fun? We have a bit of time to spare." He made the overture confident of the answer. Neither Sky nor Lexi were programmed to actually say no. In fact, they were programmed to immediately respond in the affirmative, but only to Lucas or Ramsey. Sometimes it was too easy, and Lucas thought a little "hard to get" modification could be in order one day. It might spice things up a bit. Maybe he would talk to Ramsey about that. He wasn't really sure how the modifications to Sky and Lexi were done, but Ramsey had hinted to him at how they were designed. The *brains* of Sky and Lexi were so more advanced than humans that a human communication system was built into them. Ramsey had explained it to Lucas as similar to a governor-like device used in the old days of automobiles to control the speed of a powerful engine. Sometimes he wondered how powerful that engine inside them was. Occasionally, he got hints when they needed to use it.

"Jay, play some dancing music," Lucas ordered. The BlueJay began playing a familiar tune with a good groove. Lucas approved and began to dance a little bit. Sky and Lexi walked slowly over to him while seductively dancing to the rhythm. The three danced for a few minutes before Lexi grabbed Lucas's hand.

"Let's go, my darling," she said seductively as she guided Lucas back into the portable shelter in which he had just slept.

"Can't wait," added Sky. Lucas raised his eyebrows twice at both of them as he headed toward the bubble, a portable inflatable sleeping structure they always carried with them. He called to Jay.

"Jay, keep an eye on things, will ya?" This meant Jay would have to monitor their surroundings himself for a while. Jay understood, and the music faded. The trio then disappeared for about 30 minutes. Outside, all remained quiet. Shortly after reemerging, they headed north for their destination near Yellowstone.

THE COUNCIL OF FIVE

The guests were to arrive soon, so Ramsey was seated at his normal spot at the head of the great table that sat between the staircase and the porch. The discussion this evening would be simple. The proposed cut to GAP by the Harmonians, the only income most residents of Hope had, would not be tolerated. Promises had been made and lives were built around those promises. Ramsey would be suggesting using *all means necessary* to resist. He had tried to work through normal government channels, but came to realize it was useless. The politicians on the Hope side were all just corrupt fools who obviously were on the take. Their latest reform plan was clearly born in Harmony despite their thinly disguised sales pitch. And within the federal government, there was no longer a chance of finding and electing a candidate who would assist Hope in any way.

On the back of the stairwell was a giant projection wall. It was activated when a guest arrived. Ramsey saw it was Kai Kalini, one of Ramsey's best friends. Kai had worked with Ramsey at HARE many years earlier as a sales executive, and they had stayed in contact since then. Kai was recognized by the monitoring system and the door opened. He entered and headed toward Ramsey. Kai would always notice the portrait of Kamehameha the Great, the founder and first ruler of the Kingdom of Hawaii, which always gave him comfort. He and Ramsey greeted each other warmly.

Kai was one of the most recognizable figures in Hawaii, long an extremely divided place. Ramsey and Kai efforts to provide more stability had failed. Kai was now 68 years old and resided on the Big

Island, which was now part of Hope because it could accommodate the most Gappers. This also allowed the Harmonians to occupy the legendary beachfronts in Maui and the other smaller islands with a worry-free existence absent of crime or poverty. Most people on the Big Island had managed to carve out a fairly decent existence, but the cuts to GAP would certainly change all of that. Kai was never going to give in. He had hoped a few years ago that things would go the other way. He and Ramsey and others proposed for a huge tax on billionaires that would subsidize the Hope Zone. That option went down in flames, and now they were just fighting to keep what they had. Kai knew his Island, the only one they had left to native Hawaiians, was in deep trouble. Crime had picked up in the last few years and was catching up with the rest of Hope. The Harmonians' land grab would continue, Kai and others felt, leaving them only the peaks of Mauna Kea and Mauna Lai. Maybe, Kai thought bitterly, the Harmonians would just push them all inside Volcanoes National Park to live on the edge of an active volcano.

"Kai, sit by me," Ramsey said. "I'll need you nearby if things get out of hand."

"Of course I'll do what I can," Kai chuckled, "but you know some of these folks are going to be a bit on edge tonight. We'll see what happens. I think perhaps I will be, too."

Next to arrive was Bill Johnson from Philadelphia. He lobbied on behalf of the Mid Atlantic and Northeast. He was a very tall and stylish — a boisterous but nonetheless likeable fellow who stood out in a crowd. People would follow and want to be around him. Ramsey saw this in him right away. His mixed race of African, Irish, English, and Italian made him an everyman. Though race had been a more important issue 40 or 50 years before, the more divisive and unifying factor now was financial. It didn't hurt, though, that Bill's ethnic background could help eliminate any thoughts of bias or favoritism among the voting people if at some point he was positioned as a political leader. America was becoming a great melting pot, especially in Hope, and Bill was a perfect representation of that. Bill entered the room, and all but bellowed, "Hello, my friends!" Ramsey and Kai rose to greet him.

Shortly after, Selma Lago from Miami and Claire Peterson from Wisconsin arrived together. They had managed to become close friends despite their vastly different backgrounds. Selma was born in Cuba and came to the U.S. at age 7. She was 30 now, and had seen enough of the nation's empty promises. Her parents, humble shopkeepers on their native island, had come here in 2052 with great hope and dreams for her to have a better life than they had in Cuba. Their disappointments were now hers. She had watched them listen and follow others only to be betrayed. No more, she thought when she joined the Council of Five. Same as the others, the biggest issues were the absence of land, jobs and opportunity. Just the GAP check, nothing else. Many just took it, dulled their senses with alcohol and drugs while waiting for the next payment. Meanwhile falling further and further behind. Selma wasn't one of those people, but she was close with many who were. Always at the top of her mind was her determination to fight for them. Claire, on the other hand, was a descendent of many generations of Midwesterner farmers who had created stable, productive lives through hard work. That was all over now. Their standard of living began to erode earlier in the century, but now there was no way to get it back. There was just no hard work or any work, for that matter, to be found.

The five took their places around the large table. Though Ramsey was clearly in charge, there was no official president — all had an equal say and the odd number of representatives was by design: no voting deadlocks. Ramsey had also kept the group small for a reason: big groups were usually unproductive. The Hope legislature was a perfect example and their failure was the reason the Council of Five existed. Though arguments would sometimes rage on deep into the night, they would always accept the three-vote majority and break in peace. But everyone knew that could change now as the future was so uncertain.

"All right, now that everyone is here, and we've had a chance to get reacquainted, let's get down to business," Ramsey told the group, huddled near the end of the massive table so all could hear. "I've called you all here to discuss our next course of action. As you are all aware, the federal government is being run by Harmonians, and our supposed representatives are either incompetent, selling us out, or both. Our future is in serious jeopardy. We continue to get weaker politically, and under the latest proposals we'll be collectively even poorer than we are now. We need to fight back. If we don't, our land will continue to shrink, and we'll be in the same situation as Native Americans were over 200 years ago. Hope will become a giant reservation of hopelessness." He paused to let the irony sink in. "Pun intended."

"So, I'm here to tell all of you it's here, unfortunately, it's here. We knew it was coming." They all knew what *it* meant, but Ramsey needed to make sure. "The revolution, the civil war, whatever you want to call it. Maybe we'll make up a new term. We've done each of those other things once before. We're here to begin *that*.

"Anyone here who does not agree with this as the starting point for our meeting and our position going forward needs to let me know now. We all will have a say, and this is a democracy, but I need to make sure we all have this common understanding. There is no more time for negotiations and compromise."

Selma stood, picking up her glass in acknowledgment. The others quickly followed, including Ramsey. He leaned in with his glass raised high in the air and spoke louder than he had all evening, "For the good of humanity!" The others joined in, all clinking their glasses. "For the good of humanity!"

Then they were silent, taking in what they had just agreed to. After they were all seated, Ramsey continued, more quietly. "Now," he said. "We just need to figure out how we do it. Any suggestions?" he said almost comically as he looked around the table knowing there would be.

"OK, since you asked," said Selma, in an aggressive mood as usual. "Yes, I do. You set the tone, Ramsey, now I want to further set expectations.

"I am not here for another peaceful revolution. We've done that. We've done that too many times to mention. They need to hurt and maybe some of them need to be dead. They need to fear us or we'll never get them to listen. We live in a constant state of fear from violent crime, and they live in a protected utopia."

Bill chimed in. "Yes, no more peace. You can call me Robespierre." To illustrate that, he outstretched his arms with open hands. His reference to the French Revolution provocateur was not surprising to anyone at the table. Bill was a history teacher and scholar with great passion for his subject. The mere mention of someone from that historical event did push the edge, though. They could all feel the discussion moving ever closer to advocating violence.

Kai tried the quell the bloodthirsty implication. "OK, hold on. We may be getting a bit ahead of ourselves. We're all angry, but we need to make sure we stay levelheaded about this. Referencing one of the bloodiest revolutions in history is not productive, and is inflammatory at best."

"How is that inflammatory?" Bill said. "What we're seeing now is very similar, and my reference to Robespierre very accurate."

Claire tried to lighten the mood. "I prefer calling you Bill. Much easier to say."

Ramsey jumped back in. "OK, OK. My opening remarks were not to get us all up in arms and at each other's throats, just to set the expectation and get agreement that we're entering a new phase. From the comments and looks on everyone's faces, it seems we're there. Now let's get to the facts."

"Screen!" he called out, and one dropped down, covering the glass adjacent to the back patio. Ramsey rose and stood next to the display, which faced inward from the back side of the house to prevent peering eyes from drones or otherwise. Keeping his activities and communications secret was a constant battle and focus for Ramsey. In fact, he probably spent more time on that than anything else.

"Zone Map 2069," he said next, and a map instantly appeared on the screen displaying the two zones in the U.S. from seven years earlier. "As you can see and as everyone knows, our zone was actually larger seven years ago. They have used various tactics to expand their borders, forcing people to move out to Hope or to stay in Harmony and try to survive without their GAP — not much of a choice."

The map then showed the Harmonians new territory highlighted in red. "So this is their expansion, *officially*; however, this is not even the biggest issue we have."

The map changed again to display the two zones with additional colors. "This is the same map from 2069, again just seven years ago, with highlighting in yellow to show the land within Hope owned by Harmonians back then," Ramsey said, pointing to the land within Hope along the Harmonian border with some light yellow shading. After allowing them all a moment to carefully examine the data, Ramsey swiped along the screen to show another overlay. This time deep orange and red colors were added in many areas.

"And now, look how this has changed dramatically in only seven years," he said, pointing to the deep coloring, which was mostly along the border with Harmony. "These are the cities and towns they will obviously take over next. It's a lot of land and it's frightening. If this continues, we're finished.

We'll be completely dependent on them, and to Bill's point, we're headed on a path back hundreds of years in the past. The progress of man. For some, but not most. This, of course, is happening in places all over the world. It's particularly ironic that it's happening in Europe again."

The screen quickly displayed a European version of the map. The concept of GAP incentive zones, although first implemented in the U.S., had spread throughout the world and had been intended to help the poor and left behind. It wasn't working. Ramsey switched the map back to the U.S.

Claire spoke up. "So, you're saying their next targets are the really deep orange and reddish sections, correct?" Ramsey nodded, and Claire continued. "Right, so I see in my home area of Milwaukee, the number of Harmonians moving in is particularly striking; in Texas there; and in North Carolina, near Charlotte. So, they'll be moving the wall soon, and basically taking my home away from me?"

"Exactly!" Ramsey said. "Once they get the right amount of property in those areas, they'll vote out the GAP and adjust the wall, effectively seizing more territory from us. And yes, I'm sad to say unfortunately your home will likely no longer be a part of Hope, either, Claire, and you'll be forced to either try to live in Harmony with no GAP or move out."

"Where does this end? When we're all crowded into small reservations, poor and starving?" Bill said dejectedly.

Ramsey nodded. "They seem to be paying very high prices for the land in Hope, so the sellers think they're getting a great deal. It doesn't seem as good once land and home prices go through the roof. Once the rumors begin that the location would switch over to Harmony, where property values are obviously dramatically higher, many of the locals have already sold. And then their community and all the people they knew are soon gone. And with the latest virtual technology they can readjust the wall in under a month."

They had all been educated about virtual wall technology over the past few years and now the technology was constantly visible if someone resided along the border. It looked like an actual physical wall made of stone, cement, or whatever other material desired. There was no way to climb or penetrate the wall since you couldn't actually get all the way to it. It contained a repulsive field that grew stronger as you moved closer. When you were within a few feet or so it was like trying to swim against the current of a raging river. It was also easy to move it around existing structures, which was done quite often so it looked like a giant crooked barrier. Technology had made it easy to initiate and adjust border walls around the world, so the realization that the horrible scenario Ramsey had just outlined might happen very quickly was demonstrated by the dropped jaws and stunned looks on the council members' faces. No one spoke; they just nodded slowly, acknowledging this reality.

Ramsey wrapped up the discussion. "And your former homes will become new little worlds within their giant theme park. So that's what we need to stop right now, and I have a plan to do just that. In fact, the man who will lead this effort on the ground is on his way here right now."

RAMSEY AND LUCAS

Lucas and his team arrived at Ramsey's at 10 a.m. the day after the Council members left. Ramsey never wanted any of them to meet Lucas or even know who he was. It was better to travel in the morning than at night when the government had a higher concentration of drones and robotic cops monitoring things. Mid-night travel was similar to leaving the bar right at closing time back in the early 20th Century: Very risky. Lucas entered the great room and saw Ramsey sitting in his familiar spot.

"Morning, Tim. Coffee?" he said softly still using a morning voice. Ramsey was pretty much the only one who ever dared to called him Tim, but he would only do that occasionally.

"Sure," replied Lucas. One of Ramsey's humanoids hustled over with a cup. Of course, the coffee was already made to Lucas's liking via facial recognition. Lucas didn't mind its use here as he knew the information stayed with Ramsey. Facial recognition was one of the huge problems Lucas had in concealing his whereabouts. Most people were recognized hundreds of times per day, and their steps could be retraced from almost any day of their lives. This was obviously an issue for outlaws like Lucas.

"Are the ladies downstairs preparing for their modifications?" Ramsey asked.

"Yes. I assume you can do all of them?"

"The list looked fine to me. I'll go down after we meet and make sure it's all correct. Let's step out back on the porch. Beautiful day out there. I just can't get enough of it. Especially this time of year."

Ramsey's favorite time at his mountain retreat was late spring and summer. It wasn't quite that time yet, but the cool breezes and abundant sunshine here always just made him feel excited to be alive. They both peered out to the forest and the creek below. "Well, Lucas, thanks for coming. I trust you're well?"

"Not bad, you know how I get. Always looking for something to do but try not get myself into too much trouble. We spent a few weeks at the beach in Mexico last month. I always feel inconspicuous there. I could probably use some work, though. It will feel good to do something."

"Yeah, I know what you mean," Ramsey said. "I need to do something productive every day, too."

"You're always doing something Ramsey. I know you"

"Yeah, yeah, but I mean do something meaningful. I feel like I've tried, but I'm spinning my wheels. Or even going in reverse. I can't just let what's happening, happen. There are very few people like me in this world. I don't mean people that have the will to change things, but also the means. So, I feel an immense responsibility."

"OK, Mr. Responsibility, since I'm your evil twin, what *irresponsible* thing can I help you with?"

Ramsey chuckled, and veered around the question.

"Automation for everyone. A robot in every kitchen. Time to enjoy the finer things. All empty promises. Now they're saying, 'You're having too many kids. It's my land now — move.' The GAP zone is going to be shrinking since they have been buying it up. There's nothing left to buy in their world so they're taking our lands. So, yeah, we might need to act a bit irresponsibly. I don't have any other options. After we go back inside let's take a look at the map. I need to show you a few things and we need to decide where you're going."

"Sure let's do that, but I always wonder. Why do you even care, Ramsey? I mean about these Gappers? You have absolutely everything: great wealth, success and power. Meanwhile, you're risking it all by associating with people like me. Fighting for change and even actually living over here. Why don't you just sit back and relax? Go to an island paradise? I might if I were you."

"It's empty once you've done that for a while. You start to think, 'Why me? Why do I have so much and these other people have absolutely nothing?' Their safety on a daily basis is not even assured. More importantly, how can they ever get anything when people don't work, for the most part? And I'll tell you what, my guilt is deeper. I had a great deal to do with all of this."

Ramsey paused, deep in thought.

"When your father and I were young, we were going to change the world. Technology was going to make everything better for *everyone*. Well, it didn't happen that way, of course, but it could have. Too much greed, even my own. Although I did dabble in philanthropy from time to time, it was never at the expense of my own personal gain. It was just a way to fend off the guilt. When I would meet with your dad he would bring it back to me, he was my conscience. I didn't listen enough, though, and now even he's been gone so long, but I still hear his voice."

"You know," Lucas said, "I still kind of hate him for bringing me into this world, but I've slowly been getting over it since his death. I guess maybe I've unleashed enough anger out there already to punish everyone in the world for me being born a dwarf. I still don't know why he chose to have me, though, when the world had moved to gene selection. Perfect humans. Meanwhile, I'm like the last freak on Earth."

"That's not true, of course. I know it wasn't easy growing up where you did. Hey, I know you stood out. I get why you left and changed your name. All of that. He never blamed you for that, either. You wanted to go to a place where you fit in. You made a name for yourself, though a notorious one, obviously."

"Well, it's kind of convenient for us now, isn't it? I don't think anyone has ever figured out we're related, and I don't think they ever will. In terms of HARE and your guilt, my response is that it was gonna happen, anyway. If you and HARE didn't dominate, another company would have. It was just a matter of time and the next phase of human existence."

"I don't disagree. It doesn't change the fact that I feel responsible."

"So, what's the end game, Ramsey? How do you get real change? How do you go from where we are now, fighting to just keep what we have, to a permanent improvement? Real *Hope?*"

"We need to even out the wealth and reunite. There's no other way. What you had before shouldn't matter. I plan to give it all away once we win this fight."

"Are you a *communist,* Ramsey?" Lucas said, emphasizing the word. "That's so anti-American."

"Those 'isms' don't matter anymore, Lucas. For example, what went wrong with the great communist experiment of the 20th Century, the Soviet Union? Human productivity suffered, eventually bringing down the whole state. It took some very bad actors to even keep it going as long as it did. So does human productivity even matter anymore? Software, automation, robots, and humanoids account for 90 percent of our productivity now.

"We need a new ism, something that focuses on our existence among these manufactured beings, call it Humanism. We once had such a movement, but it's faded. We can redefine what it means and take over. We need a system that focuses on the humans. We need to make sure everyone has a decent standard of living, and an opportunity to thrive, all without the worry of the downward spiral due to plunging human productivity."

Lucas was impressed. "Wow. Well said, as always, Ramsey. Lofty goals indeed. I wonder if even you have the resources and influence to make this happen."

"I have some other things in the works that I'll share with you later, Lucas. I'm not playing some short-term game here with no plan to win. Obviously, we're really starting from scratch. We don't even have a resistance. You know how in all the old movies there is some established secret resistance to whatever oppression is going on? In a story like that it's always so easy to tell the good guys from the bad. The greedy rich power seekers against the oppressed. Plus, the bad guys always go out of their way to inflict additional misery simply for their own pleasure. Those characters were always so one dimensional, and it's so easy to take sides in that setting. Well, in our reality, it's just not that simple. There's no central figure to rally against, no bad guy. It's just happening over time. Harmonians look out for themselves, and as a byproduct the lives of people over here slowly get worse. Everyone else is asleep. We need to wake them up, but it can't come from us. It must be from them. The Harmonians need to wake them up by becoming the bad guy. So that's mission one. I need you to be the provocateur and we're going to create a bad guy so we can start a movement."

"I'm game," Lucas said.

Ramsey knew he would be. They planned their first mission for the next several hours.

THE SHOW

It had been a week since Eli met up with his dad's old friend Ramsey. Eli couldn't stop thinking about the encounter. He didn't know why, but deep down somewhere within him he *did* know. He was desperate for something to change in his life, and he sensed that Ramsey represented that. Eli tried to put those thoughts out of his mind, though, as he had plans for this Saturday night. He was off because the venue his was working had managed to book another, and higher-profile act. Still, he felt things were going fairly well at his shows, though attendance was sporadic. But if enough people saw him, they would spread the word. At least that's what he hoped. Eli and his fiancé Marilyn were headed to Bay Amphitheater for another kind of concert. The venue was beautiful and in a fabulous location right on the water. They were excited to be going out together. Marilyn had been so busy with her career that they had not been able to spend too much time together. Because Eli had struggled with his, their relationship had some uneasiness about it. Although Eli would never need to worry about money due to his father's tremendous wealth, he was somewhat jealous of Marilyn because she had apparently found her calling, although Eli would never admit that.

Marilyn and Eli were the same age and had met at Berkley. Their first contact was not in class since they had vastly different curriculum, but instead at a social event. They did have something very much in common, though, as Marilyn was studying the field Eli had rejected, humanoid design. Marilyn was passionate about it and clearly talented. Their connection had started with a sort of friction:

Eli wanted to be a musician, and Marilyn wanted to build imitation ones to replace people like Eli. At least that's the way Eli saw it. This led long debates lasting deep into the night, turning an initial attraction into a much more meaningful and lasting relationship. It had been four years since they had met, and perhaps both of them felt that their bond was now being tested like never before. It was an important night for the two of them.

Eli and Marilyn arrived as the main attraction was coming onstage. They had heard great reviews and were pretty excited. Both of them were fond of 20th Century music. The band came out on stage to a loud ovation. The music began to play. It was a song called *The Tax Man*.

It sounded great. It was almost as if you were transported back more than 100 years and were seeing the 1970s band, the Kinks, live. They sounded and looked exactly like the original human band. This was the norm now. Technology had come that far. Although Eli enjoyed the performance, he also had a sick feeling. How could he ever compete with this? It was almost perfection. Bottling the greatest things and preserving them at their finest moment. A snapshot in time that could be replicated repeatedly without the decay of age. A clearly non-human thing. And what always raced through his mind, and made it worse, was that his father had everything to do with this. He didn't think it was good thing, even though it looked and sounded great.

It was an enjoyable evening, nonetheless, and both Eli and Marilyn were both having a fantastic time. As the evening progressed there was great anticipation for the finale which everyone had been talking about. The wide center aisle in front of the stage lit up in all red lights with white stars. The group launched into the song "Celluloid Heroes", where long dead celebrities are described as they walked down Hollywood Boulevard.

Then, numerous celebrities appeared, and mingled among the audience. Eli and everyone else knew they were replicas built specifically for this show to match the people referenced in the song.

Replicas built by HARE. For anyone who knew history (or had heard about the show, for that matter), the first was Greta Garbo. She was spectacularly dressed and looked like the great star she was. She looked so astonishingly real. It brought some almost to tears as the song continued.

Next came Rudolph Valentino, and his impeccable attire and larger-than-life presence that was equally awe-inspiring. It was as if each one of them had come out from their Hollywood star and lived again. Although people had become somewhat accustomed to humanoid replicas, seeing ones of Mickey Rooney and George Sanders was a truly different experience. They were rare and some-how more spectacular. Maybe because they were stars from so long ago or perhaps it was just the context. And when Marilyn Monroe came out, Eli's Marilyn could not contain her tears any longer as the words rang out. After all, she had been named after her.

There was a feeling of amazement and sadness all at once. The long dead icons being replicated and paraded in front of Eli could never have imagined this future. What is our future, though, Eli wondered? He felt at that moment that his grasp on reality was growing even weaker, and it had never, ever, been firm.

Before heading home, Eli and Marilyn mingled with their var-ious Harmonian acquaintances. Eli's fake sincerity with these peo-ple who were supposed to be their friends annoyed Marilyn. He just seemed to be withdrawing from their life. She didn't know how to fix him, get him right, although she wanted to dearly. She loved Eli, but she didn't know if she could save him from himself. Their short flight home in an air taxi was in silence. Although they had been connect-ing better at the show, hope was fading that it was a lasting effect.

PHILADELPHIA

Bill Johnson awoke as Ramsey and Lucas were meeting. Unlike the rest of the Council, Bill actually lived and worked in Harmony, in Philadelphia, which had become a popular tourist destination. When the zones were being created, it was one of those areas that could have gone either way. Government officials at the time decided that the home of the Founding Fathers had to be part of Harmony, and so they lobbied to make that a reality. As part of this lobbying effort, they also created a detailed plan to remake the city just like it appeared in 1776. The plan ended up being brilliant and worked extremely well. With humanoid replicas of the Founding Fathers all over the town, it did feel like you went back in time. Icons such as Ben Franklin and Thomas Jefferson debated in every pub. All of downtown was restored and converted to Colonial Philadelphia. Of course, there was plenty of room to build this right in the middle of downtown, as the office buildings built in the late 20th and early 21st centuries were torn down. People simply never worked in office buildings anymore. So Center City Philadelphia now looked as it had almost 300 years earlier when the great idea of America was born. Considering the state of present day America, it was quite ironic.

Bill, though, did not think of himself as a Harmonian. It turned out that one of the few jobs remaining for humans was as a teacher, and the only teaching jobs were in Harmony. Harmonians wanted humans to teach their small children instead of humanoids. There was something humans could provide young children which was extremely important — the human touch. For now at least,

Harmonians paid handsomely for this skill. The pay was so much higher than GAP, it was feasible for teachers to live in Harmony and maintain a decent lifestyle.

It was a coup for the Council to have a member living in Harmony. Bill could get a good feel for his neighbors. Ramsey did travel there quite a bit, but he didn't live and work there all the time, so Bill's insight was essential. Ramsey had worked with Bill's father at the same company before HARE was founded, though at vastly different levels. Ramsey had always treated everyone as equals, so it wasn't odd for Ramsey to befriend someone who worked in the mail room. That bond was critical in deciding whether to add Bill to the Council without the fear of betrayal. Initially, there were doubters. Council members wondered why a Harmonian would want to represent and fight for Hope. He quickly earned their trust, though. Just by listening to him you could tell he was a man of honesty and conviction. He had a deep-seeded hatred of the wealthy Harmonians thanks to his impoverished upbringing. Many people from his childhood were now dead, including his parents and many of his friends. His mother, who died young, might be alive today had she been given access to new medicines generated after the quantum computing revolution, which cured almost everything. Also, beneath his mostly pleasant life as a Harmonian, Bill knew he was eventually was going to be forced out. He quietly tracked the progress being made by HARE in early education humanoid design, and they were getting very close to finalizing new humanoid models who could replicate the human interaction Bill and other humans like him provided. It was only a matter of time before Bill would lose his job and have no choice but to move out of Harmony and accept GAP. He did love Philadelphia in its present form, though, even though it was fake. He wished he could find a way to make this real — not just here, but across the U.S. He knew that's what the Founding Fathers would want, and this made him feel like one of them. It helped him justify his mission and the unpleasant things he would now need to do.

The next morning was Saturday, and since Bill was off there was no time to waste. Ramsey had given them all a deadline and because he had to work next week, he had less time than the others. He would travel over to Hope today in his Air Enabled Vehicle, a low-cost Falcon model, to do some research and meet with friends. The journey over to Hope was not far at all but was a bit of a hassle. You couldn't fly across the border so he would have to stay on the ground and get in line. The gate at the foot of the Ben Franklin Bridge led the way, but the delays there could be up to an hour. The questioning and processing were similar to entering another country. Bill had relatives and friends in Hope, so he made the journey often. Of course, everything you did was tracked and stored by the government. About 20 years earlier it became mandatory for every citizen to have their retina registered for identity purposes. The retina scanners at the wall instantly brought up your info for the border guards who were of various humanoid models. There were only six models in total so you could get to *know* them. They intentionally did have unique personalities. The Harmony government who provided the humanoids wanted to have a warm inviting side, especially for tourists coming into Harmony from Hope or other countries. For Bill, though, it was always the same. The questions were on the order of 'Why do you need to make so many trips back and forth to Hope'? Blah, blah, blah. He knew the questions, and, depending on which guard he got, the follow up ones, too. He got through today in about 30 minutes.

Once in Hope, Bill headed to the Camden County property office. He would be researching recent property sales in order to develop Harmonian residential targets, namely, non-Gappers who had recently bought property in this portion of Hope next to Philadelphia. Each of the Council members would be undertaking a similar task in their areas. There was certain information that could only be obtained locally due to privacy protections. Bill would have to be careful, though, as his journey was tracked, and the time he spent in the property office would be on video. The Council knew this, so each of their missions would end up with an action, such as making an offer to buy a property. While researching the details of that "purchase," they would all secure the real information that they would feed to Ramsey. If detectives happened to investigate the history at these facilities after the Council actions were undertaken, they would see that Bill and the others were there for a legitimate purpose. A perfect cover, they hoped. After an hour of research, Bill secured the information needed to develop their targets while also getting enough info on the property he would inquire about purchasing. Mission accomplished.

Bill stopped in to the Colonial Lounge to meet his friends for lunch. This area of Hope was very nice compared to the rest of Hope as it was close to the Philadelphia border gate that allowed passage in between Harmony and Hope. The Hope restaurants tried to take advantage of the location by mimicking the same Colonial American theme as Philadelphia. The idea was that Gappers could get nearly the same experience at a lower cost without the hassle and expense of going through the gate. The Colonial was the top place and had the most replicas. Bill sat at the bar and ordered a drink.

"Morning Breeze," said Bill to the bartender who was none other than Betsy Ross herself.

"Certainly, sir", she said. The drink appeared in seconds.

A Morning Breeze was part of the guilt-free drink class that promised no ill effects the next day. All the drinks in this class had similar-sounding names that drove home the message of a pleasant post over indulgence experience. Synthetic alcohol, invented in 2028 and perfected with mass distribution by the late 2030s, was the key ingredient. It was supposed to cure all the ills of alcoholics everywhere. With limited long-term health effects and short-term hangover issues, people could have their cake and eat it too. What no one realized was that many people after prolonged use would fall into an almost constant vegetative state. "If it makes me feel good and isn't killing me, why ever be sober?" was the predominant theme. Most people no longer worked so essentially had no reason to wake up, especially people in Hope. After his drink arrived, Bill was interrupted by a man to his right.

"Hey, how you doing?" the man said, bumping Bill slightly while extending his hand. "I'm Don. Say, where do pencils come from?"

"I don't know, Don. Where do they come from?" Bill said. He knew the joke but thought playing along was the fastest way to get this over with.

"Pencilvannia!" Don said with glee.

"Great one, Don, Thanks. I'm meeting some friends here, so I don't have time for this right now."

"OK, have a great day, sir!" Don said, turning to a new audience nearby.

Bill knew Don was a humanoid comedian hired by the restaurant. They were becoming more and more common to generate fun and atmosphere within establishments. People like Bill, who lived in a tourist area, were tired of them. It was sort of like having a different used car salesman show up all the time and sit next to you. At least you could tell it was one of them and decide whether to engage by using the code word, their name. They usually didn't look alike, but they were all named Don — or Donna. People had complained about the intrusion, so they had standardized this method to allow you to tell. Bill acknowledged some of their jokes were pretty funny, and some of these fake comedians were better than others, so perhaps a good one could actually be a lot of fun. One of his friends had hired two for a party with pretty good results, which Bill thought made some sense. Pretty good ice breaker.

Bill took a few sips of his drink, then turned to the door to see his friends Al and Maxine enter. They were both dressed up, which was unusual. Al wore a navy sport coat and jeans while Maxine had on a red dress. Quite a stunning couple, they were. It was clear they were headed over to Harmony after seeing Bill. Meeting them was part of his mission, although they would never know. They had no idea Bill was on the Council or even that the Council existed. No one did except the Council itself and Lucas. Bill stood up and waived.

"Hey, guys. Over here!" Bill yelled. The couple walked over to Bill and took a seat next to him at the bar. Betsy quickly appeared and they ordered. Bill then quickly got down to business.

"I'm thinking of getting some property over here. I've been looking and I might have found a place. I just want to get your thoughts since it's in your neck of the woods, on Westfield Avenue."

"Well, that's not really our neighborhood," Maxine said. "Too rich for my blood. I don't know how those people can afford to live there."

"We're not that far," Al added, almost defensively. "It is really pricey over there, Bill. Our property value has gone up quite a bit because we're in the next town over. People are moving into our neighborhood because they are making a fortune by selling their houses. They're getting out now while prices are high. Especially with the GAP maybe being cut down, which is goddamn ridiculous, by the way," he said. "Wait, how the hell can you afford that neighborhood? Sorry, Bill. Are you leaving Harmony and coming here? What happened?"

"No, no, nothing like that. It's really a good thing. Things are going well at the school. I got a bump up and a bonus. It was a surprise, so I'm trying to take advantage of it. You never know what can happen in the future. I can't afford to buy a better place in Harmony so I figured I would look for something In Hope. Close enough to me. I know people and it's actually really getting nicer and nicer in this location by the gate."

This was all a lie, but Bill's friends seemed to be buying it.

"OK. Gotcha, Bill. So what did you want to know?" Al said.

And that was it. Bill had opened the door to the right conversation. Al and Maxine told Bill all about their neighbors, especially the new people who had moved in. They discussed the type of people going out to the restaurants, including this one. Bill could tell that Al and Maxine thought they knew why he was asking. He even threw in subtle hints to lead them there. Of course, he wanted to know that it was safe there, they thought. They all knew he would not have the same security level as Harmony, but with the place so close to the gate it was almost as safe. It certainly was lately because Harmonians had moved here. The line of questioning made perfect sense to them. So, they tried to convince him of the safeness of this location in Hope, all the while giving Bill the exact info Ramsey needed. They were really nice people and Bill felt a little guilty. He worried a bit about their safety, but Ramsey had assured him and all the others that there would be no collateral damage.

After 30 minutes, they exchanged farewells. Bill then returned to his home in Harmony and sent the information to Ramsey using an encoded message that could not be deciphered by the Harmonian or federal government. Even if they had intercepted the message and it was traced back to him it would look like a cabin reservation in Yellowstone. Ramsey was pretty darn crafty, and this helped ease Bill's concerns. He did worry some, though, and most of the time fretted over why things were so confusing all the time. He really just wanted a peaceful, simple existence. A life people had here hundreds of years ago. He knew he would never find it, though. From his window, Bill saw a Colonial woman sweeping the porch at the market across the street. She had a pleasant, warm look about her. At least the humanoids seem happy, he thought, and chuckled to himself.

HAWAII

Kai Kalini's home in Kona on the Big Island was in one of the nicest areas in all of Hope. The Harmonians had so generously offered, as Kai often put it, to leave some of their beautiful island paradise to Hawaiians. When the Hope Zone was created with the increased GAP, it became clear that people from the continental U.S. were planning to flock to the Big Island when they heard it was going to become part of Hope. Hawaiians knew they had to do something about it, and that's how Kai wound up getting into the political arena. They had to pretty much keep out non-Hawaiian people unless they already lived there or were being displaced from one of the other Islands. Kai initially had mixed feelings about this: it was almost like doing the same thing as the Harmonians were doing to them. He needed to protect his people first, though, as they had been kicked around too much. If native Hawaiians were all going to be pushed to the Big Island, he was going to make sure it didn't just become an overcrowded, poverty-stricken wasteland. He and others worked tirelessly to fight for the locals, and their efforts had paid off. With the population controls and building restrictions, the Big Island still remained beautiful for native Hawaiians. Kai continued to worry, though. Harmonians still had their eyes on this island and would slowly push him and the others right into the Kilauea crater, if possible. Unlike the continental U.S., Hawaii had no virtual wall. Kai insisted he would die before allowing Harmonians to gain a foothold and put any wall on this island, though there were signs of them doing just that. He was going to find out who was responsible, and he was certain Ramsey would find a way to teach them a lesson. Kai would not have to go far to find evidence as the Harmonians' foothold would be right here in Kona and up along the Northwest coast. It was just too convenient. He knew it was coming. The Harmonians were going to try to take over part of the Big Island.

So, he took a drive to collect the evidence he needed. He reached the area just north of Waialua Beach and slowly drove by a posh residence that had recently been sold. He saw a man standing on the property who was clearly not of Hawaiian decent. He was tall, likely of white European descent, and donned a Hawaiian shirt typical of tourists. Kai decided to stop and try to 'welcome' the new resident. He stopped his car, got out and waived to the man.

"Aloha!" Kai said, while waiving his hand and walking toward the man, who promptly turned his back and began to walk the other way, near the rear of the home.

"Not interested, thanks," he mumbled before disappearing behind some foliage. Kai stood there for a few minutes, irritated. He wanted to follow the man and give him a quick lesson on how Hawaiians were supposed to treat other people. Especially their neighbors. He didn't want to start any trouble, so he calmed down and decided to drive away. He knew the address, though, and it was definitely going to Ramsey. This guy will be taught a lesson one way or another, Kai thought.

ELI'S MUSIC

Eli arrived at Real Singers lounge 30 minutes before he was about to start his third week. The crowds had increased a bit, but not enough to give him any security. Eli liked how he had been performing, though, so he was going to keep at it. Rather than play covers, he played his original songs. He just didn't see a point in playing covers, considering all the replica bands out there. The owner had asked him to mix some in to get the audience engaged, but he never felt comfortable doing it. He was now playing his recently written concept album called "The Story of Henry Hopkins," which was about a fictional character from the Greatest Generation. Most people he spoke to thought it was creative and the songs well written, but it was just hard to get a lot of people to listen long enough to really take in the whole story. Eli thought he did have some fans, as there were occasionally repeat attendees in the audience. The main character in his story, Henry, had lived in the U.S. for pretty much the entire 20th century, and each song represented a meaningful moment in every decade of his life. Like the story goes for that generation, Henry had survived the Great Depression and fought in World War II. He even had a son drafted to go to Vietnam. To Eli, the story of the people Henry represented was so inspiring, the accompanying music should resonate with most people. It did with some, like the ones who showed up and asked him afterwards about the songs. He wondered if others just didn't care to even take the time to feel and understand a character like that. This thought made him sad at times, not for him, but for all those people like Henry who had died for them to live in their resistance-free world of Harmony. They had never known suffering or conflict, so maybe it made sense that they couldn't relate. Eli also wondered that perhaps he just thought too much and should just go with the flow. At times he would think that perhaps he should try to be more like them, try to fit in better. Maybe write a song about a wild, all-night party and then play it along with other lousy cover songs. That's what everyone else around here seemed to do. It all felt so empty to him, and he just couldn't. He needed a purpose and Henry at least gave him something to latch on to.

Eli was finishing his last song, in which Henry wonders about his future before taking his last breath.

> I wonder where I'm going now
> Tried to find the answers in every town
> I looked up in the sky to find a way
> Still don't know the answer here today

As Eli finished to sporadic applause, he looked at the audience and thought maybe the song was about him as much as Henry. Where the hell was he going? As the people filtered out and he began to pack up his things, he saw the owner, Dylan, approaching.

"Hey, Eli. Can you come into my office?"

"Sure," Eli said then added under his breath sarcastically, "Can't wait," Many prior discussions didn't go well. This was certain to be another one. He looked at Dylan. "Should I sit down?"

"Don't bother, I need to move on. This was your last night."

"I have a six-week contract. You can't just cut it off," Eli said defiantly.

"I'll pay you out. It just isn't working. I'll eat the money. I need to get people in here."

"Goddammit, Dylan, I don't want or need your money. Go to hell."

"Yeah, I know, rich boy. Why don't you open your own place and subject everyone to your boring music? Or pay them to show up? Maybe the Gappers would do it since they've got nothing better to do. Your dad will never run out of money, so you can just pay people forever." Dylan looked at his desk and the schedule, already focusing on replacing Eli.

"Thanks so much," Eli offered sarcastically as he turned and left. For a second, he thought he would break down. I'm a grown man, he thought, and kept it together. He really didn't have anything to say. Dylan had given him a chance after all, and Eli had failed. He was hurt most of all by the "boring music" remark. He tried to blank out all his emotions as he left the theater and headed home.

After a show, Eli would normally have an AEV taxi waiting for him to fly across the Bay and drop him off, but since he left early, he decided to walk over to the taxi stand, about a half a mile away. He needed some fresh air, anyway, and some time to clear his head. He felt boxed in, cornered with nowhere to go. What would he do now? As he walked down the street, he could see replicas through the glass windows performing various tasks to close up for the day. He noticed James Cagney's face just as he turned out the lights in James Cagney's Hat Shop. Eli shook his head and chuckled. This place is ridiculous. I've got to get out of here. I can't take it anymore.

He walked a few more steps and suddenly it came to him: Ramsey. Ramsey lived in Hope. Maybe I could pay him a visit. Perhaps I would be happier in Hope. Or maybe I just need to get out of here for a while or I wonder if I'll just feel better in the morning. Ten minutes later he made it home and went straight to bed. When he woke up the next morning, he didn't feel a whole lot different and wasted the entire day thinking about what he was going to do next. By 6 p.m. he was eager for someone to come home because he really needed to talk, to anyone. He was upstairs when he heard his father enter the home and soon after heard clinking glass. He knew his dad had just poured a glass of scotch and sat down in his usual spot at the mahogany table. He figured he would join him and see if he could find a way to tell him about being let go. He walked down the stairs and heard the sound of a news feed that his father must have just initiated. As Eli walked into the room, he noticed some kind of trouble being broadcast on the video feed, probably in Hope.

"Hi, Eli," Jack said as Eli entered the room. Suddenly he realized that Eli should have left for work already. "Wait, aren't you supposed to have left already for tonight's show?"

"Yeah," Eli said sheepishly. He figured he would just get it out. "They let me go before the six weeks was up. He said I wasn't bringing in enough people. So much for an extension."

Jack shook his head.

"They never give you enough time. It takes a while for new music to catch on. Why don't they get that? They just want to keep playing 100-year old songs that everyone knows. Doesn't anyone want to hear anything new?"

"Like you, Dad?" What about John Lennon? Isn't that the same thing?"

"That's not fair. You know I've always loved the Beatles and John."

"Exactly, it is fair. That's what people want. That's what *you* want. No one cares about hearing *new* music, or seeing *new* actors, or *new* anything. We're just a society of perfect lazy tourists getting more washed out by the day."

"Oh, I see where this is going. It's my fault. My company did this and I ruined society? I ruined your life. We'll let me tell you this. You can do *anything* you want, literally anything. I told you I would buy you a venue if you still want to do this music thing."

"This music thing? Really, is that what you just called it?" Eli said as he grabbed himself a glass of Scotch. "Now I really need a drink. The great passion of my life is 'a thing' or maybe 'a phase,' Dad? I know that's what you're thinking. You've always thought: He'll get past this phase and be like me. He'll take over my kingdom. Well, no thanks. And you just can't pay for me to have a career. Are you going to pay people to come, too? No one here cares. I need to leave here. I need to go to a place where they do."

"What? Like there?" Jack said, pointing toward the screen showing some sort of riot occurring in Hope.

"Yeah, well why not? I've got nothing to lose."

"Are you really, seriously, considering going there? Nothing to lose? How about your life? You could lose that. How about Marilyn? How about us, your mother and me. All we do is love you and want what's best for you. And you want to run off and maybe get yourself killed? You have *everything* to look forward to. This is ridiculous."

"Yeah that's me. Always ridiculous. Well, you don't know what it's like to be me. Facing this future. This pointless empty life. I need to find some meaning, whether it kills me or not." Eli gulped down the rest of his Scotch.

"I'm not giving you any money to go over there. You'll never last. What are you going to do live on — GAP? Besides the fact that it's so unethical to take that money with all that we have, you can barely make it on that."

"No, Dad, all that *you* have, not *we*. It's so convenient how you switch back and forth from me to *we* when it suits your argument. So let's try to agree on one thing. When you talk about *your* money please use the term *me*, because I never want any of it. So you can stop throwing it in my face. I'll be out of here soon and stop eating all your food, too. Give me a couple of days to gather and make plans and I'll be out of your hair."

"You can't do this to your mother. She'll be home soon. You need to talk to her and you'll change your mind. We'll just continue to argue and I don't want to do this with you."

"That won't change a thing. I made up my mind last night. The decision has been made, so I will tell her, but it won't be a discussion. I'll let her know just like I did you."

Eli headed upstairs. Stunned, Jack could not believe what he had heard. He poured another drink and sat there, wondering how he could stop Eli from pursuing this craziness.

MILWAUKEE

Claire Peterson arrived home from the meeting with the Council to her less-than-exciting life on the outskirts of Milwaukee. Unlike Bill Johnson, she had no job awaiting her. This made the days seem long, though the mornings and evenings were very busy with raising her daughter Mia. Her husband Richard was no longer in the picture and seemingly had no interest in either Claire or Mia. Claire had been too independent for Richard who became jealous and controlling at some point after their marriage. There were signs of this early in their relationship, but it had grown much worse in later years. At first, she just thought that he loved her so much that he wanted to protect her, but it had come to the point where he questioned all her activities, causing them to argue constantly. This went on for a couple of years and then all the sudden the jealousy just stopped. He didn't seem to care anymore, and Claire suspected he was having an affair. One night her suspicions proved correct, but she was astonished to find out with whom Richard was having the affair. She came home to find Richard and that humanoid, now his current "wife", in bed together. Later she found out he had used their money to secretly purchase the humanoid companion to replace her, and he had apparently been hiding this humanoid for months. With their previous jobs and now GAP they never would have been able to save enough, but she concluded Richard must have hidden from Claire some of the money he inherited from his parents to buy her humanoid replacement. Unlike a secret girlfriend, Richard could just stash this thing in the trunk or a closet somewhere, so he was able to keep it from her for a while. Even though she kept up every room in the house, Claire never did figure out where the hell Richard had hidden the humanoid. To Claire, this was the ultimate betrayal — being left for something manufactured. So, not only was she not good enough for him, even humans weren't.

After their divorce, Claire was angry and bitter toward Richard because of the new law on alimony— no one had to pay it. Because few people worked, most people in Hope lived off their monthly GAP money. If one parent split and left the financial burden on the other, there was no legal recourse. Of course, the high costs of raising a child for a career, with college expenses and the like, were no longer a concern. Plus, children would get their own check at age 18, making it less of a problem. This didn't help with the real difficulties for Claire and people like her. What was worse for her in particular was the embarrassment that Richard had put on the family. He had left them for a humanoid and everyone knew it. Plus, Richard now could have everything he wanted from a woman without dealing with her emotions and rules. Although it was happening more and more frequently, Richard was one of the first anyone in their neighborhood had heard about, and people still remembered. She could tell by the looks of pity she still received from her passing neighbors. Worry about yourself, she would think; you're probably next.

Like all the other Council members, Claire was assigned to find potential Harmonian targets. It was clear that the Harmonians were pushing north past the Illinois-Wisconsin border. The division there had been quite simple, directly along the state line allowing the residents of the posh suburbs north of Chicago to remain in their homes. Most of the people from inner city Chicago headed south across the Harmony border into Hope to get their GAP since they were not up for the deep chill of Wisconsin. Because Claire and the others besides Bill lived in Hope, their mission was easier. No border crossings meant less tracking and a slimmer chance anything would be linked to them.

Today Claire would be "shopping" for a new home in Kenosha, Wisconsin, a town sure to turn over, based on Ramsey's map. She arrived at the county records building mid-morning. It was a large building, perhaps 100 years or older. It had large white columns and a grandiose entrance designed for a time when such buildings were much more important. The size of the building alone meant great volumes of county files were once stored here. After everyone converted fully to digital records (of course, government was the last to do so), paper had gone away completely. As a result, many counties had just torn down or repurposed these types of buildings for private use. This particular one was too ornate to just be destroyed and obviously no one had tried to purchase it for conversion, at least not yet. Claire was thinking that was probably in the near future as she walked in.

"Please go to the terminal in the back and have a wonderful day," said a low-end humanoid front desk clerk.

"You, too", Claire responded in as pleasant a voice as she could muster. God, she hated humanoids. Among the crime statistics were the records of sale and who had purchased each property. Recent sales, prices, and listings were all available as digital public records online, but sometime after Hope was created and crime had spiked, the identities of the people purchasing homes were removed, along with local specific crime statistics. That was made possible through a federal law aimed at hiding how bad Hope really was, especially in certain areas. Hope had sued to make this information available, and the compromise ended up being you had to go somewhere physically and be identified to access the records. The thinking was that if you wanted to target someone for a crime, and as part of that obtaining their identity, you would not want to be on video right before this happened. Plus, if you were already a convicted criminal, you would be identified immediately and denied access. Claire obtained the names and addresses of five perfect candidates for Ramsey to target and left shortly after. She was on video the whole time, which worried her as she returned home. She was able to suppress those feelings quickly, though, as she just kept telling herself: What the hell do I have to lose, anyway? Life kind of sucks, anyhow. What really put her in a bad mood was that she kept remembering she had to have the dreaded meeting with Richard tonight to discuss getting some extra money to raise their daughter. It was never a pleasant conversation, but this time he had at least answered and agreed to meet. Claire had promised herself she would avoid digging into him about his relationship with that … thing, but she knew she might not be able to help herself. They agreed to meet for breakfast at a restaurant close to the Harmony border, where all the nicer places were.

Claire arrived on time and waited inside the lobby. After a few minutes, she saw his old blue vehicle pull up. That old piece of junk must be 15 years old by now, she thought. It was one of the models that still allowed you to sit in the front and drive yourself if you wanted to, but that had been outlawed 10 years earlier, so this feature had to be disabled. She also noticed there was someone in the back seat with him. She immediately guessed it was his humanoid. Oh my God, he brought her? She better not get out and come in here. She then witnessed them both exit the vehicle and she confirmed it was definitely her, no, *it* she told herself. It was not a woman. I cannot believe she's coming in here, Claire thought, turning toward the hostess stand, pretending not to notice they had arrived. Maybe I should just punch her in the face, but Claire knew humanoids were exceptionally strong and couldn't be hurt, anyway. How do I deal with this? She heard a voice from behind her.

"Claire?"

"Yes. Hi Richard," Claire replied unenthusiastically, turning slowly toward Richard. Though both stood there, she would only make eye contact with Richard. "I thought it was only going to be you and me."

"I wanted you to meet Isabella. It's about time you two met as she's going to be involved with Mia now."

"Hi Claire," Isabella said warmly.

"What are you talking about? I don't think so. Is this a joke?"

"No. I'm going to pay you in full and keep up to date, but in exchange I want you to allow me to see Mia sometimes. I think it will be good for both of us, all of us."

"What do you mean by all of us? Her, too?" Claire said through clenched teeth.

"Let's just get a table and talk this over," Richard said, pointing to a hostess who led them to a booth. Claire sat down on one side and Richard next to Isabella on the other. Claire stared directly at Isabella for a minute, looking directly into her eyes and almost daring her for a reaction. She was looking, too, for signs of life or some reason why Richard was attracted to this. Richard tried to interrupt the uncomfortable moment.

"Claire, let's try to move past this and do what's best for our daughter. We can't keep arguing, as it doesn't change anything." Claire suddenly halted her stare down with Isabella and looked at Richard. "Go to hell, Richard," she said.

"Nice, Claire. I'm so glad I tried to reach out and mend fences."

"Mend fences? Why did you bring this thing if you really wanted to have a civil conversation with me? How could you possibly think that was a good idea?"

"Come on, Claire, please don't be so nasty to her." Before Claire could respond a human waitress showed up and interrupted. Since there were very few waitress jobs these days, she was likely the owner.

"Good morning how is everyone today? Can I take your order?"

Richard quickly replied and ordered hoping the interruption would calm Claire down. "Coffee and number two for me," he said. Claire ordered next.

"Just coffee."

"No breakfast?"

"No, I won't be here long," she said, glaring at Richard. Then she added, "Now I don't know if this will be much of a tip for you. I'm only getting a coffee, and her, well, she's one of those things, so I don't think she'll be needing anything. I think they can do some sort of fake eating thing so maybe she'll do that. But that's kind of a waste of money, isn't it, Richard?"

"Oh, OK, I see what's going on. I'll be back soon with your order," the waitress said before exiting the scene as quickly as possible. Richard sat there angrily and was about to speak, but Claire wasn't finished and looked directly at Isabella again.

"If you're not a thing, say something Isabella. Can't you even make every day chatter? 'How about are you enjoying the weather, Claire?' Or, 'Nice sweater. I love that color, Claire.'"

"I really do like your earrings," Isabella replied. "They're quite pretty on you. And they do match your sweater quite nicely."

"Well thanks so much, Isabella." Claire said, her voice dripping with sarcasm. "How do you pick your outfits? Does Richard dress you?"

"Claire! That's enough. It's rude and you're making her upset," Richard said.

"Upset? Upset, really?" Claire shifted her eyes over to Richard and then back to Isabella a few times. All the sudden she detected a noticeable difference in Isabella's expression. Her face clearly now had a look of sadness. Claire stared directly at her again and now it looked as if her eyes were watering. She couldn't believe what she was seeing. The watering eyes turned into a few streaming tears. "Oh you have got to be kidding me. Was that a command Richard? Did you say *upset* and she just cried for you? Perfect! That is what you always wanted from me and now you have it. Congratulations!" Claire's voice had risen to the point everyone in the restaurant could hear.

"No Claire, that's not even close. You're being outrageous."

Claire got up. "Don't even bother trying to contact me again, Richard. I don't want or need any of your goddam money. Mia and I will do just fine and I'm keeping her as far away as possible from this bizarre life that you've created."

She stormed out of the restaurant and jumped in her vehicle to go home and see her daughter. During the ride home she just couldn't stop the tears from flowing. She was angry that Richard had made her cry, too. Why do I even care anymore?

MIAMI

Selma Lago was strikingly beautiful. Thirty years old and of Cuban descent, she was tall with long black hair, large brown eyes and other perfectly proportioned facial features that made people wonder if she might have been one of them, a humanoid. She could tell by the stares. People always looked at her, but this was different. Instead of the jealous looks from other women or the rude stares at her body she often received from most men, it was more of a curious, suspicious interrogation. She wanted to scream at them: *Yes, I'm a real person!*

Selma had always dreamed she could make it as a model. Her parents had reinforced that idea from a very young age. She had gotten some work in her late teens and early 20s, but never made it. It just seemed there was too much competition. With many fields being closed off to people because of automation and robotics, it seemed everyone crowded into a few fields like modeling. Plus, the ability to improve one's looks through procedures was incredible. She felt like everyone was as beautiful as her, but she knew they weren't real. It didn't matter to those who selected the models, though, and most of the other girls' families had more money, enabling them to open so many more doors.

By her mid-20s, Selma abandoned modeling and got a job at The HARE Corporation. They were one of the few employers still hiring people at the time, although many folks resented HARE, viewing them responsible for the lack of jobs and overall decline in the standard of living. She went into sales and was very successful. She was a sales account manager for the south Florida territory and had actually won a President's Club award for being one of the top sales performers of the year. The award included a free trip to Hawaii to celebrate with all the other winners, and, of course, many of the executives at HARE. One night while on the trip she had stayed up late at the bar with two other HARE employees, Ian and Kai. They were discussing what was happening to the country while HARE profited at everyone's expense. It seemed like an inappropriate discussion until she realized that Ian was none other than Ian Ramsey, one of the founders. Until now, Selma had only seen very formal profile photos of Ian Ramsey in corporate literature so she at first didn't make the connection to this rather casually dressed version of him. She thought perhaps he was trying to initiate more corporate responsibility. It was one of those nights where you just felt a close bond had developed, and things could change for you. Things did change after that, but not in the way Selma had expected. Within two years, her position had been eliminated. HARE had developed its own sales humanoids and tested them first as their salesforce. Only sales executives remained to manage this fleet of humanoids. She wanted to forget all about HARE until Ian Ramsey shockingly reached out to her a couple of months after she was let go. It became clear Ramsey had not been in favor of the purge and this had caused a rift between him and Jack Ritchie. The bond between Ramsey and Selma quickly grew from there until he finally told her about the Council, which she eventually joined. He obviously had trusted her because it was quite a risky move on his part. At first it seemed more like a do-good association that could open doors for her someday, especially because someone as rich and powerful as Ramsey was involved. He unmasked that disguise over time, and it became clear that Ramsey had loftier intentions — ones that bordered on illegality.

After being let go by HARE, Selma had gone into child care. It was a career that fell well below her aspirations, but she loved the kids. They were the only thing that made her excited to get out of bed each day. One of the things that made her angry though, was that even this career likely did not offer a future. She was in the same situation as Bill. At some point she knew the cost of humanoid babysitters would come down enough to make it financially viable to replace even this field. Her life was now entirely focused on her toddlers and the Council, which she now cared deeply about. She wanted things to change for her and her family. After this latest trip to see Ramsey she had quickly accomplished what she had been asked. She felt that no one had noticed her, but there was always this fear. There was just too much tracking of your entire life these days so she didn't know if she had missed anything. She also knew that this time there could be consequences as their work had entered a new phase, a violent phase. One she embraced, but also feared. Despite that, she did not hesitate in getting the information to Ramsey. She was all in.

NAMES

It was another beautiful day in Red Lodge, and Ramsey was enjoying it on his back porch. He had work to do, though, and decided to bring it outside with him. Exactly two weeks after the Council of Five meeting, Ramsey had all the data he needed so he sat down for a review. All the Council members had been successful, so they had five potential targets — 20 in all — from the various Hope regions. From that total, Ramsey would whittle the number down to four and then send the information to Lucas, who would know what to do. Ramsey did not specify the method to Lucas, just the desired outcome. Lucas would do things his own way. As Ramsey looked though the data, one thing became clear: Most of the buyers were young, and clearly getting the money from their parents. It provided the proof for what Ramsey suspected all along: Harmonians were waging a land grab for their offspring. It was probably just speculation to them. Something to do. A conquest of sorts. Very much the kind of thing people did earlier in the century in urban areas. Try to target the next up-and-coming area in a high crime district and flip it to a trendy hip place once a critical mass had acquired enough property. Ramsey had seen this happen in New York and New Jersey. Although that was also a displacement of the poor, this was more sinister to him. It was clearly coordinated and most importantly it would result in a wall being moved and land being seized by what amounted to another country at this point. It was like tanks rolling in and soldiers planting their flags. If they have no tanks or soldiers, why are we letting them get away with this? We *aren't,* Ramsey resolved, as his anger spiked for a moment.

Ramsey took only 30 minutes to select the properties. Some of the chosen were based on familiar, well-known Harmonian family names. Ramsey knew some of the other names due to his business dealings at HARE. The buyers were young, second and third generation heirs who were perfect candidates for Ramsey to target. He was able to ascertain a few other similar profiles and was quickly all set. The details would be in Lucas' hands by the next morning.

THE TRIP TO TOWN

Lucas had been spending the past few weeks at one of his safe houses along the Mexican border near El Paso in the foothills of the Black Range. He was waiting for word from Ramsey on the mission. The house they currently occupied was a modest dwelling on a working cattle ranch. The ranch was staffed with robot ranchers, all the same model, which made the place extremely boring. There was enough lawlessness down here near the border that Lucas felt confident he could roam out from time to time without fear of being captured. Anyway, Lucas and his ladies likely would have more firepower than anyone they would run up against.

"Hey, ladies," Lucas said. "I'm sick of this place. What do you say we get out of here and roam around El Paso for a while? We could stir up a bit of trouble, but not *too* much. We do have to do this thing for Ramsey soon so I can't mess that up." This was one of those times he wanted some resistance from Sky and Lexi, but he knew what was coming. They always agreed with him.

"Whatever you want, doll," Sky said in her usual seductive voice. "You know I can get pretty rambunctious myself." Lucas wasn't sure about that though. Did she really, he wondered?

"Yeah, fun, fun!" added Lexi. "I'm up for a bit of trouble, my darling."

"Let's do it," said Lucas as he rose. The group got dressed up for the occasion and quickly left the house to begin a somewhat risky mission of finding some entertainment for Lucas. They would take the BlueJay and could be in the closest town within a few minutes. The

BlueJay was always ready and at times like a fourth person to them. Jay was more skilled than Lucas, Sky, or Lexi in terms of what the artificial intelligence program within did best, navigation. They jumped into the BlueJay, and as they did, Lucas just said, "We're going to town, Jay."

"OK," Jay said. "Might I recommend seeing "The David," which begins in about an hour? It's very unusual for this kind of show to be in Hope. It was a special arrangement and you're kind of fortunate that it's here at this moment."

"You know what? I kind of like that idea. I've heard that's pretty amazing," Lucas said, his interest authentic. "Since I don't think I'll be getting to Florence anytime soon, or ever, I might just want to see the closest thing before one of those fake coppers takes me out. Plus, it's always good to get a bit of culture in before just settling down at a pub and getting wrecked all day. Let's go see just how good this Michelangelo imposter is."

"Perfect, sir," replied Jay, and they zoomed off. The ride would take just a few minutes. Lucas stared out the windows at the desert terrain below. He always liked the desert for some reason. It had a forbidden, menacing feel that he was always attracted to. He had a bit of that in him too he thought, amusing himself momentarily. Both Sky and Lexi were peering out the windows as well. At these moments he would wonder what was going on inside their heads. Were they just information gathering or was there more? Were they wondering about something like he was or at the very least appreciating a cactus? He knew them, but he didn't *really* know them. What he knew was the external product. The outward projection. He didn't understand what the internal processing was like to make that happen. He knew there was definitely still something missing in this manufactured relationship compared to human-to-human interaction. It was that moment when you stared at someone you had been with for a long time and could tell what they were thinking, and you could almost say it for them. He never felt that with Sky or Lexi. He could never tell what they were thinking because they never appeared to be doing that at all. Their responses were too quick, and too easy, to even try to detect that moment. One thing that he was also noticing more and more recently was that they were each doing the same thing as each other all the time, and it kind of annoyed him. I need them to be at least a little different, he thought. That was another checklist item for Ramsey.

"Where are you going to drop us, Jay?" Lucas said. "We've got to keep out of sight and kind of mosey on in, you know."

"Yes sir, Lucas," Jay said with a bit of a sarcastic tone. Jay had a bit of personality built into him which had a learning feature making him more like his owners as time went on. "I can drop you guys at the edge of town about one mile from the show."

"I could use a bit of exercise. That works, Jay," Lucas said. A minute later Jay slowed down quickly and cruised at slow pace while picking a place to land. They were still in the open desert, but civilization was close by. Jay found a spot free of cacti and dropped smoothly to the ground. The door, which also served as a ramp, opened and the three walked out.

"See you soon, friends," Jay said, closing the ramp and taking off. The three immediately could see El Paso town center off in the distance. Some structures and roads were visible straight ahead. Within a few minutes they had reached one of those roads and a building. The area they had come upon was dilapidated and abandoned. This was not uncommon to see in Hope. People had generally gravitated toward the inner cities where the infrastructure was not crumbling. Roads, bridges, power, and water systems were maintained by government robots and since Hope simply did not have enough to go around, they focused improvements on major population centers. This clearly wasn't going to change anytime soon, particularly in the current political climate. Since Harmony, as the people there put it, *paid for everything* in Hope, and constantly complained about it, more infrastructure funding was just not coming. Virtually everyone in Hope lived on GAP and it was untaxed. It just didn't make sense to provide a government income and then take a portion back to fund government. Although this made sense from a logistics standpoint the arrangement allowed Harmonians to back up their political stance. Ultimately, it was true that Harmonians paid for all government services and this reality made it increasingly difficult for Gappers to win political battles.

The group passed a few more abandoned areas before seeing a few people talking in a group along one of the roads. The buildings were becoming more condensed and this appeared to be an area where some people lived, although it really didn't look much more habitable. As they drew closer it was clear that the three people talking were all men, and perhaps could stir up some trouble, which would not be a surprise in the remote areas of present-day Hope. In reality, it would be a surprise if they didn't. There was really nothing to stop them out here. They all appeared to be nursing some sort of drink, likely homemade moonshine. There was no money out here for the synthetic stuff, and by the looks of them, these men likely didn't care too much about their health. By the time Lucas and company had come within a few hundred feet, the men had turned and clearly noticed them. Lucas and team were always quite a sight to see, but to appear out of nowhere in a place like this, with the striking beauty of the two women and the short stature of Lucas, was perhaps the most peculiar thing these men had ever seen. Lucas walked in the center of the two women wearing his usual cowboy hat and wearing a long black coat which at times scraped the ground. Sky and Lexi both wore very stylish cowboy hats and boots as always because it's what appealed to Lucas.

The men stared them down as they drew nearer, and upon closer inspection you could see their clothing was as old and worn as the area they inhabited. One of the men spoke. "Well, well, well. What have we here? You folks are clearly lost, so why don't you come on over here and we can help you find your way?" The tallest of the three men took a step in their direction. And his tone suggested he felt he may have just stumbled upon easy prey.

Lucas replied, "We're going to see The David show. I hear it's fabulous. We'll be able to get there just fine." The men started to slowly cross the street and to walk in the same direction as them. It was obvious they weren't going to get away without a confrontation. As they inched closer, Lucas raised his hand and opened his palm. "Stop right there, turn around, and go back to doing what you were doing!"

"OK, sure," said the second man, who appeared to be just a smaller version of the first.

"Sky, your turn," said Lucas. Sky quickly turned towards the men while Lucas and Lexi continued along, clearly in no distress about what was to take place behind them.

"Hey, you handsome devils. Do you want to have a party?" Sky said in a sultry voice as the men closed to within 10 feet of her.

"Now, that's more like it. Yes, we do, as a matter of fact," said the tall man, half smiling and exposing his brownish yellow rotting teeth. "It looks like you and your sister over there dressed up for us, too. I like me some cowgirls. We're going to have to ditch that ugly midget over there, though. No one wants to party with him. I can take care of him for you. Is he holding you ladies hostage?"

Lucas overheard and suddenly turned exposing his long pistols on each side of his waist.

"Changed my mind," Lucas said, drawing both guns simultaneously and firing three bullets from each. All three men ended up with a bullet in the chest and forehead before any could draw their own weapons. "Now, that was badass," said Lucas, chuckling and symbolically blowing non-existent smoke away from the pistols. He had seen that in an old western. "Never saw a trifecta of scumbags who deserved it more. What a waste of oxygen. You know we're technically on their side here, but, geez, if this is what we're fighting for? I don't know maybe we should just go back down to Mexico?"

"I like Mexico," Sky said.

"I was just kidding, Sky."

"OK. I like New Mexico, too."

"No, you don't. No one does. That's why I can just shoot people in broad daylight and no one notices." Lucas raised his pistols in
the air then dropped them swiftly into his holsters. "Let's go find some
more people to shoot."

He turned and started toward town again. "Just kidding. Don't
shoot anybody unless I tell you to, all right?"

"Got it," Sky said.

"And you, too," said Lucas as he turned and gave a stern look
at Lexi.

"Anything you say," Lexi replied almost sarcastically, which was
strange to Lucas. Sometimes he really didn't know what was going
on in there. They continued their walk to The David show, about 10
minutes away. Although he did enjoy smoking those worthless losers,
he really did hope they didn't run into any other intoxicated former
cowpokes on the way. They had left some bodies in the street, which
was a risk, but they hadn't seen anyone else around on the outskirts
of the city. The density of the structures and people were increasing,
so any conflict from here on out could cause them to abandon the
trip. There would be just too many witnesses around and at least one
person would summon the robotic coppers. Lucas really did want to
see the David show so he looked straight ahead and tried to ignore
everyone. As they walked on, the feel of poverty was everywhere.
It was written on the walls and imprinted on the faces of the people
they passed. Such desperation could lead others to approach them
with ill intentions, but there was also a lethargy there. Most didn't
seem to have the will or energy to even try. Soon, Lucas could see
the brightly lit sign, "Michelangelo's The David," at the entry to the
open-air arena. Good, Lucas thought, this is outside. The weather
is nice and there are more ways to escape. They got in the line of
about 20 people. Everyone nearby took time to stare them down.
Lucas sensed it was a "What are *these* people doing here? Are they
for real?' If you only knew, Lucas thought.

At the gate, payment was collected through a retina scan-
ner that would deduct the amount from one's currency balance.

Lucas obviously could not identify who he really was, but Ramsey had helped out with that problem. He created a retina overlay that gave Lucas a new identity with an always- available balance. They would change this identity from time to time when he visited Red Lodge. Sky and Lexi both had the same type of set up. Retina scanners could tell the difference between humans and humanoids, but Ramsey had designed them to be recognized as humans, with identities which could be changed when needed, just like Lucas. They all gained entry with no trouble. Once inside the arena, normally used for rodeos, they caught their first glance at Michelangelo himself, standing on a raised platform in the middle of the arena. It was an amazing sight. Although most people were completely unaware what the real Michelangelo looked like, it just *seemed* like him. This version was in his late 20s, sporting only a mustache instead of the thick beard he wore in his later years. The real Michelangelo spent two years sculpting The David, but this version would be done in only 90 minutes, according to the program. It was open seating, so Lucas picked a spot close to the exit. Just as they sat down, the sound of renaissance music filled the arena, setting the mood perfectly. Michelangelo had been preparing his workspace in the center of the arena and appeared as if he were almost ready. His pleated overcoat with its wide puffy sleeves and belt represented a best guess of what he would have worn at the time. He also donned a blue velvet hat designed with a brim to catch the marble shavings as he worked. He eyeballed the spectators as he walked around the plinth and the enormous marble block in the center of the raised platform. It looked as if he was judging the quality of the witnesses to his sculpting to assess their worthiness. He seemed satisfied as he nodded at the end of the inspection.

"Every block of stone has a statue inside it, and it is the task of the sculptor to discover it," he said, shouting one of Michelangelo's most famous quotes across the arena. The music slowly grew louder as he turned toward the marble. "Now, what do we have in here?" he said, facing the 20-foot-tall marble block. He extended his arms outward and opened his hands upward. As he did, a portion of the platform he was standing on began to rise. It was the inner circle that surrounded the plinth, and it was taking him to the top of the statue so he could begin carving. If you looked closely you could see his hands were not hands any longer. They now appeared to be sculpting tools. Once at the top, he addressed the audience once again. "There is no greater harm than that of time wasted, so let's begin!" Michelangelo's left hand made swift, wide-sweeping strokes across the top of the marble. Huge chunks fell from the block. This continued for about five minutes. Once he stopped, the top of the marble was roughly the size and shape of The David's head, though it had no detail. Next, he added detail with his right hand. Now, the famous statue began to reveal itself: the eyebrows, then the eyes. It was astonishing to the crowd how quickly and how perfectly detailed the statue was.

"Now that's talent," Lucas said to Sky and Lexi. "Can you do that? I mean, make beautiful statues like that? I might want some Roman cherubs around the pool or something. Maybe some gargoyles at the front door?"

"Quiet!" said a man from behind him. Lucas turned and saw an obese fellow sitting behind Sky. He gave him a nasty look, but held his temper. He returned his attention to the iconic imposter in the center of the arena. The head of the sculpture was almost complete now, and amazed murmurs came from the crowd. Lucas spoke again, louder than before, and much louder than anyone else. "That David fellow is quite a lot prettier than me. Don't you think, Lexi?" He knew he was just provoking the man behind him, and he really didn't know why. He kept telling himself he didn't want any trouble, but he just couldn't help himself he thought.

As expected, the fat man answered instead of Lexi. "Yeah, I would say so, you little freak in your cowboy outfit. Why don't you shut your face before I make you even uglier?"

"I wasn't talking to you," Lucas said, turning to look directly at the man.

"But I was talking to you," replied the man. Lucas heard and was becoming angry, but tried to control himself and enjoy the show. He did not like to be told what to do by anyone, but he buttoned up for the moment as Michelangelo worked more on the marble block. In less than fifteen minutes, a large torso emerged. Michelangelo completed the other steps before moving to his right hand to create the detail and finally polishing the torso. Now you could really see The David emerging; it was as if he was being born. Finally, as the statue neared completion Lucas turned his attention to the fat man, and decided he wasn't going to get away with his rudeness.

"Now, back to you," Lucas said. "Thanks for your patience, allowing me to witness that truly amazing sight." The man stared back at him with a puzzled, but angry look. "Sky, how about a little love tap for the gentleman?" Before the man could respond, Sky launched a sharp powerful jab to the man's mouth. His head snapped backward as his mouth spewed blood. Pretending the confrontation was over, Lucas and Sky turned their eyes back to the show, seemingly uncaring about the almost certain retaliation that was to come. Would he strike at Sky, a woman, or at Lucas, who had started it? It was almost a game they were playing with him. Michelangelo had just finished polishing The David's lower portion. The statue now glistened in the desert sun, radiating an intense brightness never seen on the original David. It was a beautiful sight to behold. As they were admiring the work, the fat man had regained his senses and decided to attack Lucas. The man stood up, wound up his right arm, then launched it forward about a foot away its target, Sky's right hand popped up out of nowhere and caught the arm, snapping it in half. The man screamed in horror. "Time to go, ladies," Lucas said. They calmly got up and walked toward the exit. But the screaming from the injured man was causing quite a commotion. Michelangelo took notice and pointed toward Lucas and the ladies as they left.

"You dare interrupt me when I'm working?" They pretended not to notice and hurried out of the exit. Lucas summoned Jay with an embedded device.

"Now, Jay! We're in trouble. Michelangelo even yelled at us." Jay showed up right in front of them with his ramp already coming down. They jumped in and took off. Lucas looked out the window and could see two robotic cops flying behind them. You could hear their loudspeaker from within Jay.

"Stop and land immediately! Now!" The command was given repeatedly.

"I can lose them by going up, so don't worry. They can't get up that high," Jay said.

"No," Lucas said. "We'll have to dispose of them. We'll be tracked otherwise. Go ahead and land. Sky and Lexi will walk out there calmly and I'll stay here. They won't know what they're up against until it's too late." Jay found an open patch, and Sky and Lexi walked down the ramp as it opened. The cops had already landed as well and were about 30 feet away, ready to strike. The robotic police were extremely skilled and difficult to defeat in this situation as they were designed to handle confrontations such as these, but with humans. Lucas didn't know how well they would fare against Ramsey's creations, and it worried him. He did have deep feelings for both, even though at first, he had tried to suppress them since it felt unnatural. Sky and Lexi walked toward the two officers.

"Down on the ground and hands behind your back," one said. "Anyone else in the craft must exit immediately. We know there's at least one more person in there." Sky and Lexi just stood there, but soon Sky spoke.

"We were attacked in the arena, sir, and were running for our lives. Our friend is injured. Can you please call an ambulance?"

"We are equipped to deal with the injured before they get to the hospital," one replied. "However, before we do that you must get on the ground now." Instead, Sky and Lexi drew pistols and fired repeatedly at the officers. Their guns could pierce robotic soldiers, the same type of guns carried by Lucas. The cops were dropped in an instant. That went pretty well, Lucas mused, but realizing the destroyed cops would have called for assistance. Potentially more problematic, the robot's webcams would have captured video on Sky and Lexi. Though they would not be identified as any known individuals, both of their video profiles would now be added to most wanted lists. Authorities also would have video of Jay.

"Let's go," Lucas said. "There'll be others here in a minute. Now we go up and out, Jay." As they took off, Lucas felt guilty about putting everyone in danger. He didn't know why he kept doing that, though. He had always needed to push the edge, even at a young age. He wondered if a human girlfriend would have stopped him. Sky and Lexi had no restraint; they did what they were told. But there was no one to calm down Lucas, to try to reason with him, to help him pick his battles. He needed that, he thought, or he was going to get himself killed. He could almost live with the thought of dying in a battle, but not for something stupid like this. He was pretty much out of control in his younger days and was lucky to be alive now. Then the thought hit him: He made it this far and now if he had to go out, it should be with a purpose. Maybe he would speak to Ramsey about some more mods to the girls to help him with his self-control. How would that work, though? Would they stop listening and obeying me, then? That wouldn't work, either. I might as well just get a human wife, he chucked to himself as he looked out at the clouds zooming past. They would be back at the ranch within a few minutes.

THE MISSION

Lucas received the details of his mission the next morning, after the risky visit to El Paso. He would use Jay extensively, as he was designed to crunch numbers, coordinates and outcomes. Everyone worked all day getting things buttoned down at the ranch as they would be gone for quite a long time. The worker robots would take care of things while they were gone, but they needed to prepare some contingency plans in case there were unexpected visitors, and not of the friendly type. After dinner, they sat down in Jay to sift through the information and determine the optimal path of their journey. Lucas still felt a little guilty about putting them all in such a horrible situation, but one of the things he liked about being with these humanoids is that they had no ability to do the same. It was human nature to expect 'looks' and snide comments after you felt you had done something wrong to a close companion, but those would never come. This he would *not* ask Ramsey to 'fix' with a modification."

"OK, so we have three places we need to hit: they're east of Philly, north of Chicago, and north of Miami. Jay, we can take you for the whole trip. Hawaii is no longer part of our planning. I know Jay you could have made it with your recent fuel cell upgrade, but we need to be finished within five days. So that's not possible. I don't know what's being planned there, but it's not our concern. So, I need you to calculate the best path that will keep us within the Hope borders and stop at all three locations."

Jay projected a digital map in front of the three and described the plan. "The best path is to begin in Miami and end up in Red

Lodge, and go to the Philadelphia and Chicago areas in between. As you can see on the map from here we'll head to north Texas near the Oklahoma border. Next, we'll travel along the southern states far away from the Harmony border along the coast, and then go through central Florida, landing on the western side of Miami."

"OK," Lucas said, "that looks right so far. I would have picked about the same route. Kind of a no brainer there. This next part of the journey is quite simple. We go back up through central Florida and straight up along the Appalachian Trail. We'll camp for the night in West Virginia. In the morning we'll head east toward Maryland, and then north through Delaware. Finally, we'll go into southern New Jersey.

"This part looks easy, but we're still getting pretty close to D.C., and there are military bases near where we're going. Camp David is there. That whole region just kind of freaks me out. I've only been there once for a reason. Seems like the heart of evil to me."

Lexi agreed. "Yeah, if we get discovered by the federal robotic soldiers, I don't think we have the firepower to protect you, Lucas, and I don't think Jay has the speed to get away. We need to be extremely careful."

"And, of course," Lucas said, pointing at Lexi, "the three of us all together are on video very recently from that scene you caused in El Paso."

"I caused? I saved your ass, Lucas. You know how to get us into things, but you need me — us —to get you out of it."

Lucas snapped back. "I could have handled those low-end coppers with one hand tied behind my back. The coppers? I could have taken them out, too. It was safer for you two, I'll give you that."

Sky chimed in. "The truth is that the cops probably would have gunned you down, Lucas. Gunned you down in the desert and used a cactus as your headstone. Then what would we have done? I don't want you to take those risks."

Lucas turned silent. Had he actually detected worry for the first time from either of them? It must have been from the latest modification, he thought. Did he even ask for that? And was the worry about *him* or *them*? He decided to probe further.

"Wow, Sky, were you actually worried about me?"

"We both were," replied Sky.

"OK, OK, I'm sorry about that," Lucas offered. It actually *was* Lucas they were concerned about. He had to concede he liked it. "I didn't mean to put you guys at risk and have you square off against those cops. You did well, though, I do have to say. In any event, that's not going to happen this time. This is business. We must be beyond careful. I'm not putting anyone at unnecessary risk, including you, Jay."

"Well, thanks so much, Timothy," Jay replied, using a sarcastic announcer-type voice.

"What did you call me?" Lucas snapped. "Never mind. Let's finish this up and get moving in the morning."

Lexi had a suggestion, "Lucas, considering that the video of your face has been blasted across Hope, and probably even in Harmony, I don't think you should be venturing out at all during this mission. Obviously, you're the boss, but please stay with Jay while we take care of each of the targets."

Sky jumped in. "And, let's face it. It would be easy to spot you for other reasons, you know like ..."

"Oh, what could those be, Sky?" Lucas said sarcastically. They all sat in silence for a moment until Lucas spoke again. "Kidding. I know. I agree too. Let's be honest: You two are built for this. Your hair color changes in twenty seconds. You can change your height. Even your facial recognition profile is never the same. Right now, if I'm spotted by myself or let alone with one of you, we're dead. You two should not even walk together. I assume you're planning to make the adjustments so you don't look anything like the girls on the video from El Paso?"

"Don't worry. We have all of that taken care of," Sky replied.

"Who said I worry about you?" Lucas needled, but got no reaction. They finished the details of their mission in a few hours and went to bed. They would leave for their trip at 6 a.m.

ELI AND RAMSEY

Considering how his relationship had deteriorated with Jack Ritchie, Ramsey was surprised by a note from Eli saying he wanted to visit Hope and Ramsey's mountain retreat. He had always liked Eli and would of course welcome him, anyway, as he had no bitterness towards Jack's family. Eli sent the note the same day he had argued with his father and left the next day. He told Marilyn that he would be gone for about a week researching material for a new musical collection. When travelling, Harmonians could just register their route once inside their vehicle and it would usually be approved within a minute. This included any travel to Hope and allowed you to skip the virtual border walls by flying right over them. Even though Red Lodge was more than 1,000 miles from San Francisco you could get there in about five hours using a typical Air Enabled Vehicle. It wasn't just the speed at over 200 miles an hour that made the journey so fast, but the ability to avoid rough terrain and go straight to your location, especially in a place like Red Lodge with mountains and dramatic land features such as Yellowstone itself along the route. When he arrived, he was recognized at the gate and met by the familiar stable of greeters that included both functional robots and humanoids. Eli found Ramsey a curious character. He immersed himself in a world of humanoids, but rejected Harmony where the entire world was built around them. As far as Eli knew, excluding the artificial beings, Ramsey lived alone here in Red Lodge. Eli arrived at the front door, which opened automatically, and he saw Ramsey waiting there to greet him. They embraced and Ramsey invited his guest to lunch on the back porch.

They walked past the American history exhibits. Eli paused several times while nodding his head. "Cool. This stuff is awesome Ramsey. I would love to get a better look later."

"Absolutely, absolutely, that's what it's there for. I've been collecting these things for so long it's nice that someone else can appreciate it occasionally. I'm not sure how long you're staying, but I'm sure you'll find some time to look at my collections," Ramey said as they passed the Texas display with some original artifacts from the battle of the Alamo. They then walked outside to the large wooden deck, and Eli quickly noticed a grand selection of fruits, meats, cheeses, nuts and berries displayed on buffet table. It looked fabulous to Eli as he did feel a bit famished. Parched as well, Eli also noticed the wine which looked delicious. They were served by two beautiful female humanoids.

"What would you like Mr. Ritchie? How should I make your plate?" said one, a black-haired, well-proportioned version.

"No, thanks. I'm a do-it-yourselfer. It looks great. I think I'll pick on my own." Eli grabbed a plate and began filling it up with a bit of almost everything from the selections.

"So, how is life over here? By *here*, I of course mean Hope, not your spectacular home. I mean, I know it's completely different than this in most of Hope. I've seen the videos but have never ventured over."

"I'm not sure why you really want to know, but we can get to that. It's not just a simple answer like *it's bad*. I personally don't spend a lot of time just hanging around the rest of Hope besides here. I do work with people who do so I can share their experiences. I wanted to take you down to the lab though first and show you a few things I'm working on. Would you be up for that?"

"You know I'm nothing like my father and I don't go to the College with him ever, so I don't have anything to share with you on what he's doing. To be honest, it's not ..."

Ramsey quickly raised his hand in the air. "No, no, not at all. I'm not looking for any information. I'm not trying to convince you to do anything, either. Just have some cool stuff I would like to show off."

"Sounds great. Sure, I'll look." Eli finished his plate and they walked inside. Most people would be excited beyond their wildest dreams for a glimpse of new innovations no other human had seen, but for Eli this type of thing had been his life since he was just a young boy. He had no expectations, but he would be polite and feign some interest out of respect for his host. Little did he know the next hour or so would change his life forever.

Ramsey led Eli to a hidden elevator on the main floor behind the Alaska exhibit. An old tin pan served as a palm reader that opened the elevator. Ramsey clearly didn't want guests just stumbling down to this area of the home. "Got to be careful these days, you know?" he said. It was more than just one flight down, so Eli knew they were going beneath the exposed walk-out basement just below the main floor. Eli supposed the bottom floor was where the humanoids had prepared their meal earlier and likely were the servants' quarters. Although he had witnessed the humanoid transformation first hand, he was still astonished at times to see it in full action. Ramsey had everything at his fingertips like an 18th century king without all the mess of the humans. He never had to pay them, feed them, and they would never revolt and chop off his head. Or maybe they will someday, Eli thought wryly. The elevator door opened.

"Oh, my!" Eli said as he stared in amazement at the enormous and brightly lit room. "This place is gigantic. It looks like a factory." As they stepped from the elevator Eli noticed the room was filled with robots and humanoids performing various tasks. It was in stark contrast to the main floor of Ramsey's home where he paid homage to a time in America which came before technology took over everyone's lives. This was today's American reality and, knowing Ramsey, some of its future, too.

"And here I thought you were out here settling down, taking it easy," Eli said. "Hah!"

"Well, I've got to keep going, Eli. Much more to do. I can never stop working."

"I mean, I know you have the company near Jackson, so I figured this was a retreat. Just your residence. I wasn't trying to infer I thought you had retired or anything."

"It's quite alright. I understand. Let me show you around. Over here is the human modification room. If you want something just let me know," Ramsey said with a wink as he pointed to a glass room. It was closed, but Eli could see in. It resembled an operating room and was likely a sterile environment. Places like this were common these days, but Eli wondered why Ramsey needed his own kind of secret one. What kind of mods was he doing?

"No, thanks, I'm feeling pretty good right now, but I'll let you know," Eli chuckled while shaking his head. They moved past the corner room to the wall along the right side of the room where there was lots of activity. The robots were building something here. It was a new humanoid of some kind. Eli couldn't tell if it was a replica of someone or some kind of companion. "OK, so what do we have here?"

"A new model. I like to innovate here before producing at the factory in Jackson. I just finished the design before you arrived. It's a warrior model."

Eli was surprised. "Those are always robotic models, right? This looks like a humanoid, and I think it's female. What's the point of building a humanoid warfighter? They cost so much more to build and repair and all they need to do is fight?"

"Maybe they should do more than fight," Ramsey said. "Maybe they could be compassionate, diplomatic, and try to avoid conflict unless absolutely necessary?" He paused for a moment then added. "I was thinking a robotic model could be programmed to do all that, but who wants to come to a peaceful resolution with a war fighting robot? With a compassionate woman, though, who seems sincere and caring, now maybe that could work?"

"Work for the purpose of whom? Unless that's something you can't share. Dad told me you had some military contracts, but that's all I know. If you can't go any deeper, I get it."

"Yeah, I do have those contracts. It could be for them. Maybe not. I don't even know if they would want or use them for their intended purpose."

"What is their intended purpose? Like a United Nations peacekeeper? I could see that," Eli said, shrugging. "When the UN replaced humans with robots, they obviously lost something."

"Do you really want to know? You can't tell anyone, including your father. Can I trust you?" Ramsey said sternly.

"I promise. Won't tell a soul," Eli said, putting his hand over his heart.

"I'm building spies. What makes them spies versus any other humanoid? Things like changing their appearance and facial recognition profile. Their profile will come back as an upstanding human each time. Right now, their design is based on three unique actual humans. By changing a setting, their faces are modified, and each shows up as a different person. They don't look exactly like the person's identity, but the important features match like shapes. You just have to know how the algorithms work."

"Oh, I guess this is where we might want to stop. I don't think I want to know anything else, and I'm guessing you can't go any further, either."

"That's probably enough for now," Ramsey said. "Let's go back upstairs; I want to show you a few more things I've been working on up there."

"Sounds good," Eli replied, a bit relieved. "Let's go."

MIAMI

"We're 30 miles away and we'll be there in less than 10 minutes." Jay broadcasted over his audio system. "Prepare for landing."

"We're ready, Jay." Lucas said as if Jay should have known. "We can all see the same thing on the map. Just use your audio only if there are any sudden changes I should know about."

"You got it, buddy," Jay said.

"Buddy? Didn't you get what I just said? Just shut up, Jay," Lucas muttered while shaking his head. He was in an anxious mood. He now turned his attention towards Sky and Lexi who had moved to each side of the bay door waiting to exit. They were completely naked since they were going to enable the cloaking features built into their skin. They only used them when absolutely necessary, like on a mission such as this. Lucas didn't want them walking around the house while completely invisible because it was bizarre, so he insisted they never use the feature without him asking them to first. They looked beautiful with or without their clothes, he thought, as they both switched on cloaking and vanished before his eyes. It was really a strange sensation, as he could almost detect something was there. Maybe it was just a memory of them being in front of him just three seconds before, but he really didn't know. Maybe it was all too much for his brain to comprehend, he thought.

Lucas would be tracking them on the virtual map. They could signal to Jay if there was trouble and Jay would relay the message to Lucas. They landed in a shopping area, about a quarter mile away from the target's house. The BlueJay touched down, and both ladies quickly exited, Sky heading right while Lexi went left. They passed opposite sides of the shopping center to reach different locations near the home. Sky would stand in front, making sure no one arrived unexpectedly. After she gave the all clear, Lexi would disable the alarm, enter the back of the house where she would plant the three devices. Lucas watched all this on the map, hoping that no one would be home, so they could just get this done and be gone. Lucas usually got a thrill out of confrontations, but this was different. He didn't have any control, and there it was again, that feeling. He couldn't deny the fact that he was worried about them. He didn't know why, though. Who is going to catch them when they're god-damn invisible?

Lexi arrived at the rear property line of the home by crossing and squeezed herself through some large thick pines that acted as a privacy fence. The only way an observer could tell something was there was from the brief movement of the trees, caused by a quick gust of wind or perhaps a squirrel. They wouldn't give it a second glance. The home was very large, almost a mansion, and appeared to be brand new. It was circled by an eight-foot-tall iron fence, which Lexi hopped with little effort. She waited in the rear of the yard to hear from Sky.

Sky walked on the other side of the street a few houses down from the targeted home to assess whether anyone was home. She was built with advanced sensory features, way beyond what was out there with most humanoid models, which she would be leveraging now to their utmost abilities. This allowed her to focus her attention on a point like a home from a significant distance to detect light, sounds, and motion. After a minute or two nothing could be detected and no cars were present, though there was a large garage separate from the home. Based on that high confidence level, she signaled to Lexi and also warned her to inspect the garage from the rear before attempting to enter. Lexi and she were networked together so they could communicate information back and forth without anyone hearing. They used a secure session to do this, and each bit of information disappeared after it was received. Though it wasn't human language-based, everything could be hacked and decrypted, so Ramsey had designed a method that essentially was not worth the effort to try to crack. Once the signal was received, Lexi would combine the data with her own analysis focused on the back side of the home. If the data matched, they would have even greater certainty that no one was home. Sky also knew Lexi could handle whatever came her way once inside. Even if someone was there, the only risk she could see was if the alarm was tripped somehow and the robot cops arrived quickly. Still, Lexi could escape right in front of their eyes while cloaked. One of them would have to physically touch her or she would need to bump into something for them to detect her presence.

Lexi got the signal from Sky, and immediately peered into the back window of the garage. She saw no vehicles, so she went to the rear door of the home and easily unlocked the door, then disabled the alarm system. Once inside, she could see the home had unusually lavish décor for Hope. She quickly found a door leading to the basement. She didn't need to turn on a light switch because she was built to see at night. All three devices would be placed underneath the home, so Lexi spent some time making sure she planted them in such a way that they would never be discovered. Within five minutes she was done. But as she neared the top of the stairs, she heard a noise. It was a male voice. She paused.

"Hello? Is someone here?" came a confused-sounding voice. "Why is this door open?"

A man walked to the stairs and looked down. Lexi could see his face, no more than eight feet away. He was disheveled, appearing to have just woken up. The man slowly closed the door. Lexi stayed quiet and listened. He was making a call.

"Hey," she could hear the man say. "Is this place haunted or something? I swear to God I just heard someone walk in and go down the basement. I come down here and see the basement door is open." He paused. "No, I didn't go down there so I don't know if someone is here. Do you think I should call the police? I don't want to make a crazy scene, but we're not in Harmony. I really feel kind of nervous." Another brief pause. Lexi wanted to make a move, but she was sure his eyes would be fixed on the door. The man continued.

"OK, OK, I will. Better safe than sorry. Bye." Lexi decided she needed to escape immediately. If he thought the place was haunted, her best move would be to confirm that. He might not want to explain to the authorities that he had just seen a ghost. She heard him begin make a voice command to call the police, and before he could make the call, she opened the basement door. The man's eyes widened in horror. Lexi decided to conjure up voices from old movies to help make the idea more real.

"Get out!" she said in a deep, evil-sounding voice as she scurried across towards the back door. "Get out!" she repeated. The man bolted toward the front door and darted outside. The plan had worked. She now had the perfect opportunity to escape out the back. She left and was quickly over the back fence and away to the road. She heard from Sky.

"What's happening? I just saw a man run out of the front of the house in pajamas."

"Yeah, someone was there. We should be fine. Meet me at the BlueJay."

The pair entered the BlueJay, and quickly got dressed. The BlueJay took off and headed north toward their next destination.

"Well how did it go?" Lucas asked.

"Yeah, Lexi, how did it go?" Sky said chidingly.

"Well not exactly as planned. Let's just say the guy that lives there probably has some new beliefs."

"What the hell does that mean, Lexi?" Lucas said. "Beliefs?"

"Yeah, like he probably believes in ghosts now," she answered.

"Oh, I can't wait to hear this," Lucas said as they made their way to West Virginia. They would be in Capon Springs in about five hours and sleep there in the bubble for the night.

HAWAII

Kai was simultaneously nervous and excited at the prospect of putting his portion of Ramsey's plan in motion. He had spent considerable time convincing Ramsey that he could handle this task own his own. Ramsey had wanted to send the same team to all locations, but getting them to Hawaii and back would add almost a week. That really wasn't the biggest problem, though. Trying to get in and out of Hawaii undetected was going to be very difficult, and Ramsey knew it. They needed someone who was already there to handle this. It had to be Kai.

He returned from Ramsey's place to Hawaii with the three devices without any problems. He knew exactly the home where they would be planted too. His recent trip had confirmed his suspicions about Harmonians moving in along the Northern coast. He didn't care all that much that the man who had ignored him on his earlier visit and was now the target had seen him. After the deed was done, someone would have to prove he was the offender, and he was going to make sure that was impossible. Plus, he had power and connections here on the Big Island. Although the Harmonians were moving in here, too, just like in continental Hope, there was more unity here among the native Hawaiians. Kai was convinced his people would help him cover his tracks without question.

The plan was for Kai to walk right into the home and plant the devices. He knew the man who had created the security and video system, and Kai had enlisted another man to develop a plan ensuring it would never be triggered nor capture him on video. Kai knew he was basically trusting this man with his life, but he was comfortable with that. Kai wouldn't tell Ramsey, who was smart enough to know that Kai had his own network. If they kept things separate, the plan would work.

After he finished breakfast, Kai got the signal that the residence was unoccupied. He arrived at the property after a short drive and easily gained access to the home. He was able to plant all three devices within 10 minutes and he was gone. It was that simple. The hard part was going to be the cover up. Since he had potentially been recognized by the homeowner who had ignored him on his earlier visit, he knew it was perhaps better for him and his security contact that the man was home when the event occurred. He felt a little guilty about that, but not too much. He really did hate that guy and people like him. He was ready for war.

JOE AND EMILY – THE DEBATE

Bill Johnson was just wrapping up a nervous weekend. He knew that Ramsey's mission had started, and he figured something would be happening in the Philadelphia area on the Hope side on Saturday or Sunday. If all was quiet, he would assume everything went according to plan. He kept his ears and eyes on all news sources to see if any strange stories appeared. There was nothing so far, so he sat down for the Sunday evening debate everyone had been waiting for.

The rhetoric between Joe, the Artificial Intelligence being who represented Hope, and Emily, the AI rep for Harmony, had been heating up recently. Their reach among the people was at an all-time high, so there was a buzz in the air in both Harmony and Hope about their public debate on the proposed cuts in GAP. Both AIs made compelling arguments. Joe appealed to keep the GAP payment intact based on human opportunity, America's history and projections of the standard of living in Hope. Emily stuck to sheer economics: GAP was extremely expensive, perhaps ultimately unsustainable. Their video messages would be seen across Harmony and Hope — projected on the border wall, on other virtual billboards, and via interruptions of various video and audio feeds that people subscribed to. A Hope resident could be watching a video on cooking, for example, and suddenly a 30-second public service announcement from Joe would interrupt the program. Each government had mandated that these feeds could be injected into programming at no cost. Of course, you would only see Emily in Harmony and Joe in Hope. It became normal to people after a while.

The supercomputer behind Joe was fed information by the Hope party, currently led by Caiden Calloway. He had several folks behind the scenes who financed the operations and had a say in Joe's content. Ramsey was one of those people, though his involvement needed to be kept secret. Ramsey also knew Caiden personally, but didn't want to get that close for fear of being exposed as a major financier. Because Ramsey had federal government contracts, his association with the Hope party would be a problem for him. So, in order to avoid direct contact, Ramsey had a couple of pass-through individuals who so far had been undetected, so he remained publicly unassociated. Lately though, no funding had arrived to Caiden from that channel. There was no way for Caiden to contact Ramsey directly, so he wondered what was going on. He feared that perhaps Ramsey had abandoned them and now supported the Harmonians. After all, in Caiden's mind Ramsey *should* have been a Harmonian, anyway.

Emily, on the other hand, was closely associated with her financiers in Harmony. Paul Bento was the party leader, and he made no bones about his place within the elite of Harmony while also serving as the elected governor. He had direct access to the facility which housed the supercomputer behind Emily. Their stance of *we're in the right* on these issues was very clear and very public. Folks like Paul frequently commented in the media and sounded virtually identical to Emily when they did.

As discussion roiled over GAP, someone on the Harmony side had the idea of a debate between the Artificial Intelligence beings, which would be fed live across Harmony and Hope. It was at first rejected by Caiden and the rest of the Hope party, as it seemed too risky. Not only did they have to win the battle of ideas, but they had to worry about Emily being superior technologically because Harmony had more skills and money to invest. Their supercomputer was simply more powerful. Behind the scenes though they continued to kick around the idea while assessing their readiness and putting even more investment into the supercomputer behind Joe. After about six months they decided they were ready and had agreed to move forward. The two sides had finalized a set of questions in advance based on a lot of back and forth negotiation. The questions included, "Is the current GAP payment fair?" and "Do the proposed GAP cuts make sense for its long-term sustainability?" Some questions on both sides had been negotiated out. One such question proposed by Hope was "How does the long term future look for residents of Hope under the proposed cuts to GAP?" This type of question would give Joe the opportunity to open the door on the glum projected standard of living argument, which was central to his normal public dialog. The debate was taking place on Sunday night when more people would be home. All screens throughout the U.S. and some abroad were broadcasting the event. Internet channels and audio sources would also take a break from their normal content for the one-hour event.

Precisely at 9 p.m. on the East Coast, Bill saw Joe appear on the left and Emily on the right of the virtual screen, their first appearance together. Joe's projected image, as everyone knew, was really that of Tom Joad from the "Grapes of Wrath." Joad was the character who spoke for poor tenant farmers during the Great Depression, but now was the political face of Hope. Emily, on the other hand, was not based on a single character, but an amalgamation of many desirable human characteristics. The main projection was of the girl next door, but smart as a whip. Her appearance most closely resembled Annie Hall from the Woody Allen movie of the 20th century. Bill was aware that Harmony had won the right to field the first question, so he focused his eyes on Emily. He listened, and as expected, it was about the fairness of the current GAP payment. She began her answer, which would be limited to one minute.

"Thank you for the question. To begin I wanted to go through a bit of history on this topic. The entire concept of GAP was created by the people of Harmony to help those without the means to gain better lives, build businesses of their own, and ultimately provide a chance to experience the American dream again. It was not really intended to be a permanent entitlement, though the generous people of Harmony are not necessarily opposed to that. As everyone is aware, the population of Hope has increased substantially over the past 10 years, and as a result the current triple payment, which went into effect around 2065, is too much of a burden on the people of Harmony. So to answer the question, 'Is it fair,' the answer is no. It's not really fair to increase the burden on the sons and daughters of Harmonians due to irresponsible population growth in Hope. In addition, the substantial funds sent to the people of Hope have largely not been used for their intended purpose. Unfortunately, most of the money has been squandered irresponsibly."

Five seconds later, Joe began his one-minute answer.

"Thank you all. I humbly speak before all Americans on this important topic. Obviously, my concern lies with the residents of Hope, but I'm really appealing to the greater good and ultimately our unity as a nation. Simply stated, the people of Hope are falling behind. Their percentage of overall wealth versus Harmonians shrinks every single year. This is due to them depending almost completely on GAP for income, which has not increased with the rate of inflation. Meanwhile, Harmonians own most of the land and businesses not only within Harmony, but in Hope as well. This situation is unsustainable, and to instead to propose a *cut* to GAP is inhumane. So, to get to the root of this question, 'is the current GAP payment fair,' the answer is that no it is not, and we seek an increase. In addition, GAP alone is clearly not enough. People of Hope seek opportunity, the ability to *accumulate* wealth, and, most of all, some reason to be optimistic about the future. So, we need increases in GAP — not cuts — and we seek greater ownership of our land and businesses."

Bill listened to Joe's response and when he finished, he put his hand on his chin and wondered. He thought the message was heartfelt, even though Joe didn't even have one. It appealed to human decency, but would it make anyone change their behavior? He shook his head and told himself no. He would watch the full hour, but he expected more of the same. This approach was never going to be enough. Ramsey had been right all along. Bill watched the entire debate and he heard nothing that changed his mind. He went to bed shortly after it was over, hoping the Ramsey business in his area would be finished by the time he woke.

JACK RITCHIE AND PAUL BENTO

Jack Ritchie happened to have a meeting scheduled with Paul Bento the morning after the debate. Jack had known Paul and his family for many years, and Jack was one of the top donors to the Harmony party. He knew Paul would want to pick his brain on how well Emily had performed, try to convince him how fantastic it was, and ask him for even more support. Jack wasn't sure he would agree, though. He was kind of sick of this whole political business and wasn't even sure the cuts in GAP were the right thing to do. He just wanted to get this over with. They would be meeting at Jack's office at the college. He heard a knock on the door, and invited in Paul.

Paul was a very tall fellow, slender, with unusually long brown hair for a man of his age. He was also extremely friendly and com- plementary, almost annoyingly so, at least to Jack. Paul got right to the point.

"Well, I'm obviously anxious to hear what you thought of Emily. I thought we did extremely well, don't you?"

"I watched. To be honest, I don't really enjoy those things. I know you want my money and I've been giving some, but I really don't want to be involved."

"But it's really important and we sincerely appreciate the sup- port. We're looking to do some more things with Emily, and I was hoping you could help out."

Jack sat there for a few minutes. He looked at Paul, turned away and looked down while putting his hand on his forehead. After what seemed like an eternity, he looked up again. He put both hands in the air as he spoke.

"Look. I really don't like this. You know, when I see Joe up there, I see me, too, in some ways. I think that's because I was a Joe at one time. Just a guy trying to make it. Dreaming and struggling, and still being able to dream. All the while, though, I knew I had the chance to make it big. Which I did and I'm proud of that, but do people in Hope honestly have that same chance? No, not really. So if you're asking me did Emily win, I'm not sure. I'm on this side, but I kind of felt for Joe. And do I feel like giving more money to get more out of Emily, the answer is no. I'm sorry to be so rude, but this is the way I feel. Now I want to get back to the lab."

"Fine, Jack. Speaking of the lab, how is the research going?"

"Very well. We're doing amazing things over there. I know you're involved in many of the same research with HAMS," Jack said. HAMS was the Human Advancement and Modernization Society and Paul was the founder. Jack had been a casual member, but some of the literature had been a bit offensive to him. It was essentially an unadvertised secret society only intended for very elite Harmonians. He didn't know what they were up to lately, but part of their mission was the extend human lifespans. That was fine to Jack, but it was the other part of the charter that made him a bit queasy. He knew Paul had asked him to see if would be willing to get more involved in the group and perhaps share his advancements. He wasn't interested and decided to once again get Paul out of his office so he could escape the HAMS questions which were sure to come.

"And I really do need to go," Jack said firmly while extending his hand to Paul who was no fool. He could tell Jack was finished and decided not to push. He didn't want to annoy him so much that he would dodge him in the future.

Paul said calmly, "Maybe can I come back in a month or so and check in on you?"

"Make it two, if you don't mind."

Paul rose out of his chair and extended his hand. "Will do. See you then and thanks for your time."

"Thanks Paul. Good luck," Jack replied as they shook hands. Paul quickly exited and Jack suddenly felt very relieved. He could feel that in some way that, at least briefly, a burden had been lifted from his mind. Paul could be a bully, even to someone like Jack. He had no idea he was going to say what he did to Paul or even that he felt that way until he said it. I kind of acted like Joe, I guess, Jack Ritchie thought to himself which amused him momentarily.

ELI - ONE MORE NIGHT

Eli awoke early in the morning with the realization he had been at Red Lodge for two weeks, and he wondered if he had overstayed his welcome. He had been enjoying the scenery and beautiful hikes most days while playing his guitar at night. He also enjoyed his evening conversations with Ramsey, whom he thought was just brilliant, and he felt if he got anything from this break it would be the knowledge he gained from just listening to him. He missed Marilyn and he expected he'd be going home soon, but the problem was: To do what? He wanted to see Marilyn and his family, but what then? What was he going to do with himself? He shook his head and got dressed. When he went downstairs, he saw Ramsey was out on the back porch, as he was most mornings, but today appeared deep in thought as he gazed out into the mountainous forest. "Just amazing, isn't it?" he said. "I never get tired of this view."

"I guess that's why I'm still here," Eli replied. "At least until you throw me out."

"I'm not throwing you out. In fact, I'm hoping you'll stay another day at least. We're having a visitor today. He's a bit of a notorious figure and you may be surprised that he's an acquaintance of mine. I trust that what you learn behind these walls stays here."

"Of course, Ramsey. Don't worry about that. Now you've piqued my curiosity. Is it someone from Harmony or here?"

"Here in Hope. I'm very involved here trying to make things better. It's behind the scenes because it can't be known. Everything turns to politics once you're involved and you must pick a side. I have interests on both sides. If it were known I was associated with Caiden and the AI Joe, it wouldn't take long until I lost my government contracts."

"But you are associated?"

"Yes, with them and this fellow you'll meet in a couple of hours. After we finish our coffee, let's go in and we can both get ready for my guests to arrive. I'll have the staff make up a nice brunch out here.

"OK, but seriously, I do need to get back. Marilyn is going to leave me. I'll hang here for one more night and then head back to the Bay Area."

CUSTER

Lucas and team had successfully placed the devices in the locations near Philadelphia and Chicago without incident. They spent the night in Custer, South Dakota. Lucas awakened at 5:30 a.m. He had chosen to stop in Custer not only because it was two hours from Red Lodge, but also because he was very fond of the Crazy Horse statue there. He was hoping to get a perfect view of the enormous carving on a bright clear morning here, one in which Crazy Horse would appear to be pointing directly at the sun. Lucas also was thinking it was nearly 200 years since the namesake of this town, General George Custer, had met his end up in Montana. Lucas wondered if they were gearing up for a big celebration; he didn't know if that was something you celebrated or not. Sitting Bull was an American, too, right? They would be going just south of the battlefield on the way to Ramsey's. It would be easy to swing by, but considering the heat they were still under from his careless trip to see The David show, he could not risk it. Plus, they needed to finish up their trip and meet with Ramsey on schedule. His thoughts were interrupted by Sky, who informed him of the time.

"Yeah, Sky, I'm awake. I was just sitting here thinking about this place. I wish we could spend some time here. I love the Black Hills. It would be great if we could take make a quick stop over to the Badlands and shoot some rattlesnakes. Nothing better than that, right? Oh well, we have work to do. I just want to at least look around for 10 minutes before we leave."

"Lexi is in the BlueJay and we're ready to go when you are."

"Tell her to come out. I want to get a few photos with my favorite chief in the background," Lucas said. Sky nodded and went to fetch Lexi. Lucas walked out of the tent and saw the Crazy Horse memorial as soon as he exited. There was not a cloud in the sky, so the photos would be perfect. He noticed Sky go into the BlueJay and it was clear she had not paused to look at the carving. It was not a surprise, but it was something he wished he could get from his companions. They didn't care about the beauty around them. How do you program that in? Maybe I'll ask Ramsey. A few seconds later Lexi and Sky exited the BlueJay together. They didn't need any time to get ready and looked perfect; human women probably hated that as much as anything about these humanoids, Lucas mused.

"OK, ladies. Come over here and let's face this way with our 200-year-old friend right behind us. I'll be in the middle. Jay, take a photo of us."

"Coming, Lucas," said Lexi as she and Sky scurried over. "We're going to look fabulous."

"Don't we always?" Sky said. "At least I do."

"Just take the picture, Jay," Lucas said, exasperated.

"Stay right there," Jay said. "Smile. Yeah, that's great. You guys look pretty sharp. I took 10 pictures real fast. Should be some good ones." The group took down the tent and loaded the BlueJay.

Jay took off five minutes later. Lucas figured he would spend most of the two hours enjoying the scenery below. They would see Devil's Tower right away and then go over the Big Horn Mountains. This area was all part of Hope so they could go where they wanted, and didn't need to be too careful as the policing up here was on request, at best. Hope just didn't have any resources to manage this area. Lucas felt most at home here and in the other areas of Hope where few people lived. As they passed over the mountains, he envisioned a home for himself along a river he had spotted below and Jay had been following. This would make a nice summer home, he thought. As the river disappeared and the terrain below shifted to a flatter high desert, Jay informed them all they were almost there.

RAMSEY'S

Jay pulled up to Ramsey's house and let Lucas and the girls out, parking in his usual spot in the garage that housed all of Ramsey's AEVs. As the group approached the front door it opened as usual since they were already recognized. Also as usual, Ramsey's warm grin was waiting for them as they entered. He quickly introduced them to Eli, who was struck by the ladies' beauty and how odd a match they were for this guy Lucas.

Ramsey led his guests toward the rear deck for brunch. Even though they had passed the artifacts many times before, Eli and Lucas paused a few times. Ramsey delighted in watching his guests take notice, so he never hurried anyone along. They reached the huge sliding doors that opened to reveal the predictably impressive spread.

"Wow, Ramsey. You sure know how to party," Lucas said, pointing to the champagne and the caviar. They all grabbed a seat. Eli noticed that the ladies he had just met were not served, which led him to wonder if they were human. He guessed not. Where was he, after all? He figured it would be confirmed shortly.

"I do know how to party, Lucas. Always up for one, even in the morning," Ramsey said, taking a sip of champagne. "But not too much. There's always work to do. I've been introducing Eli to some of my work. Some of my thoughts about what's happening here in Hope and over there where he's from." He pointed to the West.

"Pardon me, Eli. I need to speak with Lucas alone for just a minute," Ramsey said as he waived Lucas over to the corner of the deck so Eli couldn't hear. "Hey, I got your modification request for the ladies. I just wanted to speak for a minute before we send them down. Some sound a bit tricky. I may have some ideas but wanted to get your explanation."

"Thanks, Ramsey. I guess I can sum up the whole list by saying I just want them to be more real in terms of their spontaneous interactions. Not just with people, but with the world around them. I want them to strike up more conversations with me, and others. You see over there now?" Lucas pointed at Eli, who was staring from the deck to the creek below. "Eli is clearly observing nature, but they're not doing anything. Not enjoying the beautiful view you have here, or interacting with Eli. Now, if he struck up a conversation, then they're engaged. That's fine.

"So right now, I would say Sky should be taking in the water slowly rolling over the smooth rocks. Lexi should feel peace from the soft sound of the water as it cascades between those rocks and lightly splashes. Then they might make a comment to Eli about it. You see what I mean?"

"Perfect example," Ramsey said. "I think we can do something about that. Let's send them down now. The staff will get them prepped and I'll be down later."

Ramsey motioned to Sky and Lexi and whispered in Sky's ear. Both immediately headed inside as Eli approached.

"So what's your story, Eli? What do you do over in Harmony?" Lucas asked.

"I'm a musician. Folk music. I've been performing songs from my album over there for a few years. It's very difficult to get a following these days, as you can imagine. It's just a really tough business. I'm a glutton for punishment, I guess, so I've kept trying. Maybe I've just about had enough now, though. Not sure, we'll see."

"Very admirable," Lucas said.

"How about you? How do you know Ramsey?"

"Now that is a very long and sordid tale," Lucas said, shooting a look at Ramsey. "Not sure what Ramsey shared, if anything."

"Nothing yet," Ramsey said. "I'm not sure how much I want to, either. For your own good, Eli."

"OK. Yeah, you're right. I don't," Eli said, raising his hands like two stop signs. "I don't want to get mixed up in anything. I'm just a singer, man."

"Don't worry, my friend," Ramsey said. "I won't tell you anything to get you into trouble. But I can say this: Lucas and I are organizing a movement for change. It's what I've been alluding to in some of our other conversations here. Lucas is just helping me out with that. The one thing that's been very distressing to me is that Harmonians have been acquiring land in Hope with the goal of converting it over. It's not supposed to work that way, Eli. Plus, with the cuts in GAP, it's just not going to work. Someone must stand up for these people. Things are just going to get much worse."

"Yeah, I can go along with that. I've had my own struggles to be honest. The truth is that if I didn't have a rich father I would probably be living over here."

Lucas jumped in.

"And so would every other child born in the last 20 years. What could you possibly do to make a living? That whole "making a living" thing is over now. You're either born with money or you're never going to get it. There's going to have to be some kind of transfer of wealth from people like Ramsey to people here. Simple as that. If that doesn't happen, we might as well divide as a country permanently. Even if we did separate, we could never allow them to keep all of the good parts like the national parks."

"Couldn't have said it better myself, Lucas," Ramsey said.

"So, you guys want to establish a separate country?" Eli said.

"Not necessarily," Ramsey said. "The point is that either residents of Hope be given a chance to become equal Americans or we divide and establish our own country. But that is probably not going to happen as we need more of the resources they've taken and made them part of Harmony. The current path is unsustainable. Now you see the decay of Hope outside the cities: abandoned businesses and homes due to the GAP income test provision. People can earn about what GAP pays or a little more by running a small business without robotic workers. Many tried to take GAP and run a business, but they all pretty much got caught. So, they would rather take the check. The businesses close, the people move out, and you end up with modern-day ghost towns. On the other side, if you take away GAP, there's not enough jobs, not even close."

"I get it, I really do," Eli said. "I was thinking of playing my music over here for a while. I thought about it, and I'm not sure if that's even possible. I don't know how anyone would pay me. If they have enough money, they would just buy a humanoid. They don't want to keep paying someone when they can just purchase something once and be done."

"Exactly," Ramsey said, "and replicate that thinking across every single field."

"And it's all your fault, Ramsey," Lucas said, giving Ramsey a jab.

"And my father's, too," added Eli. "Don't think I don't know that. I wish you two were getting along again. With his influence, maybe he could help you. The two of you together, who knows? It's been too long. Maybe I could help. I'm going to tell him I was here, that you would like to patch things up. Is that OK?"

"Certainly is, Eli. I would absolutely embrace the chance to be friendly with your father again. Maybe enough time has passed that we can let bygones be bygones."

"I'll let you know what he says. Now let's try to have some fun and drop all this seriousness. I'll get my guitar. Do you have any drummers or bass players in the house?"

"Actually, I believe I do." Ramsey and Lucas spent much of the rest of the day listening to Eli and a makeshift humanoid band play Eli's originals as well as popular songs from the past. It took their minds off what was about to come. Eli left early the next morning.

CLAIRE

A few days after her meeting with Richard, Claire brought up the live news feed on her virtual screen. She had been nervous the past few days as she knew something was about to happen. She was just ready to get on with it whatever the consequences to her. She felt nervous for Mia and a little guilty. What if they hauled her off and Mia was sent to Richard's house and had to deal with that machine as her mother? Mia had been at a friend's house and would be home soon. She wanted her to be home when it happened, so she was anxious every time she was out of the house for a long time. Finally, the door opened.

"Hi, Mom."

"Hi, thanks for being on time. I was getting kind of bored sitting here"

"Yeah I can tell. You're watching that?" Mia pointed to the news feed. "Nothing fun there."

"Yeah, yeah, I know. But it's important to keep on top of things now and then. There's a lot going on."

"There's always a lot going on. I'm like, what can you do about it? And if you can't do anything, why bother even paying attention to ..."

Claire interrupted sharply.

"Because someone else will just take and take from you if you're not paying attention. That's why."

"Geez, OK, Mom. You sound angry all the sudden. Did you talk to Dad today?"

"Noooo! Stop it, Claire. Just trying to get you to understand that you need to pay attention. It's not always about your father. My whole life is not just about being bitter about him. I'm trying to talk to you, tell you something."

"OK. Sorry. So how was your day? I was just over at Samantha's."

"Fine. I was out shopping, but I really didn't need anything ..." Claire trailed off as she quickly turned her attention to the news feed. A breaking news emergency alert flashed. She was almost frozen with fear. The attack had happened, and she would have to deal with the consequences. The reporter began.

"Within the past five minutes, a huge explosion destroyed an enormous home in the northern suburbs of Milwaukee. We don't know if there were any people inside at the time. If anyone was home, there are no chances of survival, as the residence was leveled."

Claire was having difficulty breathing. She couldn't let Mia know, though, so she just stared straight ahead looking at the live shot of the scene and a pile of rubble.

"Similar explosions happened at the exact same time at three other locations in Hope. They are north of Kona on Hawaii's Big Island; near Miami; and in a Philadelphia suburb. As you can see in this footage, all the explosions were extremely powerful, leaving enormous craters. Had the blasts occurred at major population centers, thousands of people could have been killed. Because of the timing, authorities are calling this a terrorist attack."

"That's weird," Mia said, looking at her mother.

"Yeah," said Claire, still staring at the screen.

"It could have been worse, I guess. If you're going to set off explosions why not target a large gathering of people, like a sporting event or something?" Mia asked.

"I don't know," Claire said, slowly turning her head toward her daughter. But she did know. And she was worried. She hoped that no one was home, at least in Milwaukee. If they were, it would mean she was part of a murder. She could be a *murderer* now. She didn't know if she would ever be the same after this moment.

HAWAII

Twenty minutes after the explosions, Kai got an urgent message from the person who had shared the information with him on the now-leveled Kona residence. Kai was furious and ignored it. He really wants to talk to me now? What an idiot. He just wants to get us caught? He wished he could just tell the guy to keep quiet and stop trying to contact him, but he also didn't want to initiate any conversations that could be tracked or monitored. He was extremely worried the man would tell someone out of guilt or go to the authorities. He guessed he had to get in touch with him, so he arranged to meet with the man the next day. He had trouble sleeping that night as news of the bombings were everywhere and all anyone wanted to talk about. He had tried to seem surprised and concerned like everyone else, especially when dealing with his wife, Leilani. After he was able to finally get her to change the subject and discuss other topics, his mind eased slightly, and he eventually fell asleep. The bombings were again front and center when he awoke.

"Honey, did you hear?" Leilani said as she turned on the light while getting a news feed in her virtual reality implant. "Two people were home and killed in the bombings here. Five total people were killed. They're saying it's terrorism. They don't know or won't say who did it, though."

Kai was suddenly wide awake. His heart sank. The face of the man who had walked away from Kai flashed through his mind. He must be dead now, Kai thought.

"There were people home?"

"Yes, they found remains of a man and a woman."

"How do they know it was terrorism? Did they say?"

"No, I don't know. They must know something though. I hope they catch them soon. I still can't believe one of the bombings was here of all places, so close to us. That means the people who did this were probably right here in Kona."

"Yeah, I'm going into the government offices this morning to see what I can find out." Kai headed for the bathroom to get ready for the day. He wouldn't be meeting his contact for about two hours, but he figured he could drive around, get some coffee, and talk to a few people to find out whatever he could. He was ready in less than 20 minutes and started to leave without saying goodbye.

"Hey," Leilani said. "Are you just leaving without talking to me or even just saying anything? Do you think it's safe here? They could still be here, you know."

"I'm sorry," Kai said as stopped to give her a goodbye kiss. "It will be fine. I'm just anxious to help find out who did this and make sure it's safe."

Kai rushed out, wondering if he had made a big mistake. He didn't feel sorry for those who had died. They deserved what they got due to their unrelenting greed. He had never contemplated getting caught, though, and what it would do to Leilani. This gave him a sick feeling inside, one he now feared would never leave.

SAN FRANCISCO

A few hours after Eli returned home, he heard the news of the bombings. He thought it was strange, but didn't pay it too much attention. Who would coordinate bombings in Hope? It didn't make any sense. Some lunatic fringe group? He was sure they would be caught, though. It was impossible to cover your tracks nowadays. Probably some internal squabble within Hope. Eli's parents weren't home when he returned from Hope, but he anticipated seeing them this morning. He went downstairs and saw both his mother and father at the table.

"Hi, honey," his mother said warmly as she got up, walked over, and gave him a hug. "We really missed you. I hope you had a great trip."

"Thanks, Mom. It was nice to get away. To see some things out there that I hadn't seen before."

"You spent the whole time in Hope?" his father asked with a raised eyebrow.

"Yes, I did," Eli replied calmly. His father tried to hide his disapproval. It mostly came from his overprotective side. Now that Eli was home safe it wasn't much of a concern to him as long as he wasn't going back. Jack tried to sound positive.

"Well, it is good to see the other side. Other places in general. It makes you appreciate home, and, you know, just how lucky we all are."

"Yeah, I guess. We can talk about it later." Eli wasn't ready to tell them he stayed in a luxurious residence and didn't even get to see or understand how people in Hope lived. They would be totally shocked he had connected and stayed with Ramsey; telling them this would almost certainly lead to a confrontation. One he was not ready for.

"By the way," Jack said, "I've been feeling sick about the way we argued before you left. I'll try to be more understanding from now on."

"Thanks, Dad. Let's just try to forget about it. OK?"

"Agreed. Hey, did you hear the latest on the bombings?" Jack asked, now satisfied they had put the argument behind them.

"Well, I heard there were four explosions and a few people were killed."

"Yeah that's right. But now they've figured out who was targeted, and there's a connection among the four bombings. All the targeted residences were of people and families from here in Harmony. All four were from prominent wealthy families who had recently purchased a residence in Hope. It seemed at first that Hope was targeted. That doesn't appear to be true now. It really was an attack on Harmony. "

"Wow. That's horrible, but now it makes more sense. I was wondering who wanted to bomb some poor people in Hope. Really, though, depending on who did this, it could start up some serious trouble."

"You're not going back over there," his mother quickly interjected. "Not now. Good thing you're home already. I wanted to see you when you got back yesterday, but we had this thing we couldn't get out of. Anyway, I came into your room when we got home and saw you sleeping. I kissed your forehead. I'm still allowed to just barge in and do that you know?" She didn't expect any answer and added, "Have you seen Marilyn yet?"

"No, I will today. I was tired and she was busy, so we have plans this afternoon. It was nice to get away, take a break from everything, but I missed her, missed you guys."

"We really missed you, Eli."

"I know, Dad. I'm sorry about the way I ran out, too."

"It's fine. We're just happy you're here now." It seemed that their disagreement was now a thing of the past. Eli felt good about that as he sat down with them to eat. Something was bugging him, though. Something about the bombings. He couldn't pinpoint what it was, but it was there. He put it out of his mind for now and enjoyed the meal.

RED LODGE

The day after the bombings, Ramsey and Lucas sat in the living area next to the grand table where the Council of Five held their regular meetings. They had six virtual screens up with various local and regional news feeds. Sky and Lexi had completed their modifications and sat along with them. It was always best if Lucas could spend some time with Sky and Lexi while still in Red Lodge to see if the changes had met expectations. Lucas could definitely see a difference.

"Hey, Lucas," Sky said while sitting right up against him with her hand on his leg. "I never asked you, what's your favorite color?" Lucas stared at her for a second before replying.

"My favorite color?" He threw up his hands and then said. "OK. Gold, I guess."

"Why gold?" said Lexi who had cozied up to him on his other side. Lucas this time looked at Ramsey and raised his eyebrows.

"Because I want to be rich, like him," Lucas said, pointing at Ramsey.

"OK, mine is red," said Sky.

"I like blue," added Lexi, who continued. "Now what's your favorite song?"

Lucas again looked at Ramsey, this time with a more accusatory stare. Ramsey slowly raised both hands, and motioned for Lucas to calm down.

"Take it easy, my friend. They're trying to get to know you better. This will improve your relationship with them. You should remember their answers, too. Could come in handy on birthdays, anniversaries, if you know what I mean? I think they both might want you to be more considerate of their needs in the future. Isn't that right, Lexi?" She quickly took the bait.

"Yes, I like presents. When *is* the last time you got me anything, Lucas? Like never?"

"Wow!" exclaimed Lucas. "OK, Ramsey, can we step out on the deck for a second?"

"Sure, be right back ladies. I'm just going to give some gift-giving advice to old Lucas here. He doesn't seem very experienced."

"OK, I told you to relax," Ramsey said as soon as they walked out. "I added an advanced human emotion prototype to them. I think you'll really like it. I know it's going to be a bit different for a while."

"But I didn't ask for this ..."

"You asked them to notice the world around them more. To be more engaging with it. That means you, too," Ramsey said. "Get it? They'll need to know you better to be more conversational. And, if you know them better, they can respond with more interesting answers. Obviously, they've always had extremely advanced learning capabilities, but this mod gives them more focus on what they're learning, so they can be better friends, companions, whatever."

"That makes sense, I guess, but what about this gift thing?"

"It helps build stronger bonds. Get over it and get them something occasionally. They have more appreciation thoughts built in now too." Ramsey paused and then added. "You know what they don't have, and I should put in? Jealousy. How about I add a little of that? That would be a fun thing to watch. I hope you notice they always get along great, and you can stare at any woman you want without a reaction. There's still time before you go. What do you say should I send them down now to get the jealousy modification activated in their personalities?"

Lucas laughed.

"You're such a rotten person sometimes, Ramsey. I'm going inside." As they walked back in, they turned their attention toward the news feeds which were all focused on the explosion in Hawaii.

"Investigators have informed us that all of the targets are connected to families from Harmony," the announcer said. "This appears to be no coincidence. The chances of the small percentage of Harmonians living in Hope all being targeted randomly is extremely remote. As a result, the investigators have turned their attention toward Hope hate groups."

"Hate groups? I wonder which ones?" Ramsey said sarcastically. He couldn't think of any. Although there was a general feeling of bitterness and jealousy towards Harmony, there was no organized resistance. The only thing he could surmise was that it was the politicians they were going to go after. This could end up being quite good, he thought.

"Caiden? Joe?" Ramsey mused aloud. "They're going after the party by calling them a hate group? Maybe they're seeing this as an opportunity to further weaken the legal political opposition by demonizing them? This could work in our favor."

"Hmm," Lucas said. "Well, when do we make the next move?"

"It's their move. We wait. I'm just getting a sense now of what it could be. It might be better than I expected. We could also stir the pot a bit to lead them in the direction we want. Let me think about that."

THE PRESIDENT

After the bombings, Paul Bento, the outspoken leader of the Harmonians, received considerable pressure from the families of the victims to respond immediately. All four families targeted were connected to the Harmony party in some way, mostly financial. That made it easy for Harmonians to jump to the conclusion that the Hope party was directly responsible and should be reclassified as a terrorist organization. Two days after the bombings Paul had a meeting with federal government officials to begin the discussions on that front. He had demanded a meeting with President Emma Johansson, right in the Oval Office. The meeting was scheduled for 2 p.m., and Paul was already annoyed when a few minutes had passed. The president had better not make him wait long, he thought. Moments later, the secretary called to him, "Mr. Bento?"

Paul walked over to her. Not surprisingly, he could tell by her imperfections the secretary was a human, which was unusual to see as virtually all administrative staff were now humanoids. They couldn't have that here in the White House, though, due to fear of hacking. There was even talk of some foreign governments planning to replicate US government humanoid staff with an aim to make a switch in order to plant spies directly within the government offices. It seemed like a farfetched idea, but some had raised it.

"Go right in, Mr. Bento. The President is waiting for you."

He was extremely anxious as he entered the room, and as soon as he did, he was surprised to see guests other than the president. He quickly recognized both the Homeland Security Director

Noah Burns and Secretary of Defense Dwight Howard sitting in front of the president's desk. The mood seemed very serious to him as the President spoke.

"Hello, Paul," she said. "Please sit down over here." She pointed to the chair on Paul's left. Although she was a very attractive woman, the president made you quickly forget that fact when you met. Everyone had seen her public photos with her long flowing reddish-brown hair and stunning blue eyes. In this setting, however, she was very buttoned up and prepared. He was always impressed.

"Hello, Madame President. Certainly, thank you for meeting with me," Paul said as he sat down.

"Now, let's get right down to it," the president said. "I've been briefed by the HSD in front of me who has already met with both the directors of the CIA and FBI. As you can tell, the Secretary of Defense is also here and involved. We're taking this situation very seriously. Director Burns, why don't you start?"

"Here is what we know. The CIA thinks there's almost a zero chance it was a foreign government. The FBI director agrees, although they have no credible leads on who it really was. So, we're targeting domestic groups, seeing if they've left any digital trails. It's impossible to get around these days without us knowing about it. We're confident something will turn up. The FBI has intense focus on this issue right now. Even though we believe that the attack was from domestic sources, the CIA will continue to look externally until we're sure it's not a foreign entity. We did review the possibility that an enemy could try to divide us further using these kinds of tactics. We need to continue to rule that out."

"Thank you," said the president. "Secretary Howard?"

"Well, from my perspective I need to be sure it's not a foreign government. If it was, I would likely be recommending an immediate response, Madame President. The impact of the bombs with the enormous craters does show that these were advanced technology, which may indicate that they came from a state-sponsored terrorist. Assuming it's not and considering the nature of the attacks I have serious concerns about trusting any policing entity who is based within Hope to carry out any investigation or response. So, if you require assistance from my organization, we're ready if the order is given."

"Thank you, Mr. Secretary," the president said, turning to Paul. "Now you have the latest. I would like to get your thoughts."

"Thank you, Madame President. I'm going to get right down to what everyone I've spoken to in Harmony believes. Frankly, they think it's connected to the Hope Party. It's too much of a coincidence with what's going on with the political rhetoric to not be connected. Now I don't know if it's tied to Caiden directly. I have no evidence of that yet, but likely there is a connection to the Hope party somewhere. Who else would have a motive? I just can't come up with any other explanation. I guess there's a small chance of a foreign body like you just mentioned. The truth is that all of our enemies have so many internal issues to focus on right now I just don't see how they would even have time or motivation to concoct such an elaborate, sinister plan."

The president nodded. "Although it would be almost unfathomable if our political foes would resort to violently attacking people who disagree with them, I unfortunately believe you might be on the right track. We all know they've grown more and more radical with their ideas, and now maybe even their actions. I'm not preaching patience here. We need to take immediate action. If the other party was in any way connected, this is treasonous. I want Caiden taken in for questioning and held indefinitely until we find who's responsible.

"I also want to send troops to the main border areas. We need to demonstrate that any organized resistance will be crushed and those responsible arrested, and if convicted, executed. Furthermore, if this gets any worse, I have no issue with halting GAP payments. We'll see how well this strategy works out for them then. It just infuriates me that all they want to do is take. We're extremely generous with GAP and all they want is more. Well, maybe they'll get nothing and see how it turns out for them."

Paul was heartened by her words. "Well, I'm very pleased to hear that, and the folks in Harmony will be, too. Frankly, I can't ask for more than that, so I'll go back, and we'll wait for updates."

"Thanks for coming, Paul. We'll keep you posted," the president said, standing and extending her hand.

"My pleasure, Madame President," replied Paul as he exited.

The president was pleased; she had put on a great show for Paul. It came naturally to her at this point. When the Paul Bentos of the world were before her, she played to perfection the role she had crafted for herself.

Emma Johansson was been born into an upper-middle-class family that owned a mid-size trucking business in the Chicago area for generations. The company had reinvented itself many times, surviving good times and bad for almost 75 years. Things such as the fuel crisis of the 1970s, the financial crisis of the early 2000s, and even the invention of driverless trucks, at least initially, had not been stronger than the owners' will to survive, and mostly thrive. During the time when autonomous trucks first started taking over on mass scale in the late 2020s, the company had no choice but to take on massive debt to modernize the fleet with a more expensive line of driverless trucks. They thought their investment had paid off at first, but as the cost to manufacture the trucks fell due to robotic factories, a few giant players cornered the market and drove the smaller companies out of business. These larger companies began buying enormous lots of trucks at a volume discount and ran them on razor-thin margins until they had cornered the market. Once the Johanssons were out of business they knew that their substantial savings would eventually run out. Emma was young at the time so a career outside the family business seemed in order.

A good student, Emma decided to pursue the law. It was already becoming apparent that fewer fields would exist for humans; the law was risky, too, due to the automation of legal services and the plethora of attorneys competing for few jobs, but it was one of the better options. Once she graduated and saw the limited options out there, politics seemed like a possibility. She had gotten married young and her husband Ethan and she decided it was probably the best direction for them at the time. Her husband had gone into what seemed to be a future-proof field, but was now a clearly dying career in computer programming. Systems could learn and create other systems and programs by the 2030s, so humans were barely needed in this field at all, and only the best of the best remained employed.

Soon after Emma entered the political realm, the topic of dividing the U.S. into zones based on wealth was introduced. At first, the families who fell directly on the wealth–income borderline were angry at the concept, then realized that they should do all they could to be on the Harmonian side of the division. Emma's family was living in downtown Chicago, which would become part of Harmony. The salaries for good politicians who were willing to work hard on behalf of Harmonians were high enough to support a Harmonian lifestyle. So politics became a way for families to become Harmonians even though they didn't have the wealth of some of the others. There was one catch, though: If you wanted to stay you needed to be loyal to those who really ran Harmony. The ones with the real money who would never have to leave. Families like the Bentos and the Ritchies.

So, politics had worked out well for the Johanssons. Emma quickly rose through the Harmonian party to eventually run the Harmony Zone. It was a great living, but most days she hated it. She never liked having to represent someone else's positions even if she disagreed with them. She was constantly in meetings that made her cringe. It was the stuff of bad movies with the rich guy trying to screw the poor — only it was for real. The Harmonians also privately selected her vice president, cabinet and entire administration to ensure everyone was serving only them. Through it all, she remained publicly confident, presented a good face for the camera, and commanded great respect. Through the years, the only person who knew her real feelings was her husband Ethan, who constantly pressured her to keep the job even though she at times wanted out. She finished her day after her meeting with Paul and went to the residential side of the White House to see her husband and daughter. Ethan heard her come in.

Emma gave him a quick kiss. "I just met with Paul Bento. He wants Caiden arrested, and I agreed. I really didn't have any choice this time, but sometimes I feel like I can actually speak my mind to those people."

"I think you can, honey," Ethan said. "But you just need to be careful."

"I will. You know I will." But Emma hid the fact that she was annoyed by his comment. Ethan was always protecting himself, she thought, while he sits here and does nothing. Emma loved Ethan, but sometimes he just made her furious.

PHILADELPHIA

Bill Johnson kept his head down for a few days after the attacks. Activity was intense in his area after a young, vibrant Harmonian couple had been killed. They had just moved to Hope and came from prominent families. The families were now putting intense pressure on the authorities to capture those responsible. They had completed a conference call with Paul Bento the morning after the attack, and he had assured them the matter would be raised directly with the president. Bill thought he was safe, but you never knew what kind of government monitoring was happening that people didn't know about. Because he was a resident of Harmony, he'd be safer than the others, particularly Kai, who would be part of a smaller pool of potential suspects. Bill had traveled between the borders frequently so he did wonder if that would raise suspicions. He decided he would have breakfast at a restaurant in Harmony. He was accustomed to eating alone as he hadn't had a companion for more than five years now. The girl he had lived with for several years, whom he thought he would eventually marry, had been gone for a long time now. She had grown more and more unstable, and eventually Bill had to move on. He hadn't been able to meet anyone since. His strange existence, moving between the two zones, made it extremely difficult. He felt like he didn't fit in anywhere. Today, his plan was to sit at the counter that would provide him the best chance of striking up a conversation with another patron. He would try to listen to people's thoughts on the bombings and relay whatever he heard to Ramsey. Normally, Bill would be able to get info by just going to work and speaking with other teachers, but because of spring break, he wouldn't have that opportunity this week. The restaurant was just a block away from where he lived; he sat on a stool in the middle of the long counter. This place was still a tourist site, like everything else in his neighborhood, but it had some more unique characters than most of the other places. Specifically, it was a British loyalist establishment. He looked up to see the "owner," William Allen, one of the most famous loyalists from Colonial Philadelphia, standing in front of him.

"What are you having today, patriot? If a patriot is indeed what you are?" the humanoid William Allen said suspiciously. Bill declined to take the bait this time. He had engaged Mr. Allen on several occasions before. It was always an interesting conversation and was usually different each time. He had quite a depth to him and apparently was updated often. Bill liked hearing the other side of history, especially from a person who had grown up in Philadelphia. It was great for people to get this type of education, but it was not for him today. He had other things on his mind. He also was now struck by the irony: he was decidedly not a loyalist in the quite recent conflict.

"Coffee and the King George Breakfast," Bill said in his booming voice. William Allen nodded in acceptance. He was smart enough not to engage when he detected people were not interested. He would likely try again, though.

Bill spotted a woman three seats to his right. "Howdy, ma'am. From the area? Haven't seen you around here before."

"Oh, hi," she replied. "Yeah, actually not too far from here. Over in Gladwyne." Bill knew this was a very wealthy Main Line suburb. She would be perfect.

"What brings you into town, if you don't mind me asking?"

"No, I don't. I'm actually the mayor over there. The local mayors are gathering here today to discuss safety, you know, with the recent issues and all." Bill knew he had just struck gold potentially.

"Oh, sure," he replied. "Good idea. I'm really interested to hear what you guys are thinking. I actually teach right over there at the private school." Bill pointed, and noticed the woman's face brightened. William Allen returned and placed the food in front of him without any banter. Bill started to eat. The woman replied.

"Oh, the upper elementary. I have two kids in that age range. It's a fun time. I don't want them to get any older." She giggled a bit.

"Yeah very impressionable. That's why I like it," Bill offered, but now that he had her trust he wanted to get to his real agenda. "So do you know if there's going to be any response to keep Harmonians safer? Meaning here or over in Hope? I'm wondering if they'll restrict travel or monitor the border areas more closely. I mean the place is like the wild, wild West. Meanwhile, people have businesses over there, and we let them come over to visit us. The people that did this could be here right now in the next restaurant over, for example."

"I totally agree with you. I think we need restrictions on people coming over. The next attack could be here. And I also think we need more of our policing on their side. Let's have any conflict happen there. If this is the way they want to live we can't let that impact our families." The woman rose from her seat. "Hey, good meeting you, and good luck. Have to go."

"Pleasure to meet you, ma'am," said Bill, waving goodbye. He looked back over the counter to see William Allen standing in front of him again. He quickly finished most of his plate without engaging him. When Bill had finished eating, William Allen saw another opportunity to spark up a conversation.

"So, my good friend. What do you make of this Continental Congress group? Seems a bit treasonous to me, don't you think?"

Bill stood up. "Another time, my friend. Another time." He winked at William and proceeded out. The meeting with the woman had confirmed his feelings on a potential response. Even though it wasn't a ton of detailed info, he would relay it to Ramsey. Every little bit helps, he thought.

HAWAII

Kai spent the day after the attacks driving around, talking to people and just getting a temperature for how people felt about the bombings, and more importantly what they knew, if anything. He could tell right away everyone was in the dark, including the local police and government officials. Now he was supposed to meet his contact. Kai was extremely paranoid, so everywhere he went, he was careful to look around to see if he was being watched. He hadn't detected anything or anyone following him since he first left the house, but that didn't ease his mind. He was on his way to meet the man who could identify him to authorities and ruin him. He needed to get some sense of security out of the meeting, though that seemed a long shot. They had planned to meet at a breakfast place just south of Kona. The man was taller than Kai, younger and more muscular. Kai suspected he was one of the few people in Hawaii who still did some manual labor. The look on the man's face was threatening, too. He spoke before Kai could even say hello.

"Let's go sit down." They walked to a table in the corner, alone but for an older couple on the other side of the restaurant.

"Hey, I know you're upset," Kai said.

"Upset? You've ruined my life. Nobody told me you were going to do that. I assumed it was the normal harassment of outsiders, you know? How could I expect this? I wouldn't have gone anywhere near this thing. You're such a respected figure. I need to ask. Why? Why did you need to resort to violent criminal actions?"

Kai paused for a moment and peered out the window to gather his thoughts. He turned back and looked directly at the angry man.

"Because the way it's going, we're dead, you know," Kai said. "Once they cut GAP, we're finished. We'll get very poor and they'll just buy up anything they want. Haven't you seen the Native American reservations on the mainland U.S.? I'll die before I let that happen. These people who moved here are just invaders to me, and I'll treat them as such."

"So, it was you?"

Kai's eyes widened, and he put both hands on the edge of the table pushing himself away. He had not expected that question, but he quickly realized why it was asked. The man had already gone to the police, and their conversation was almost certainly recorded. Kai's heart sank, and he sat there in silence. Any further discussion would just provide more evidence. Kai wasn't sure what to do. Should he try to get in his car and escape? Would they just arrest him?

Before walking out, he looked at the man and said, "I don't know what you're talking about." As he opened the door, his heart sank further. At least 10 police cars rolled up, guns were drawn and Kai was ordered to get down on the ground. He dropped to his knees, then face first on the ground. He tried to appear calm, but he was panicked by the thought of his wife and family and what he had done to them.

SELMA

A few days after the bombings, Selma Lago couldn't stop thinking about them. When her shared autonomous taxi arrived, it was a relief. She was on her way to school to teach for the day, which took her mind off things and made her feel more relaxed. She had really loved the class this year and would be sad when the school year ended in a couple of months. She would miss them all terribly. Soon, a man got into the taxi in the pod next to her. The taxi was one of the most common four-person models with separate compartments for each passenger and a safety barrier between them. When autonomous taxis first began operating there had been some attacks of passengers against one another, and with no driver to assist, it became an issue. The solution was individual pods that could be joined if both parties pressed the unlock button. There were also buttons for the front and back dividers, so if a family or group of four jumped in the vehicle they would all just press the buttons removing the barrier. The pods went back to singular mode after someone exited the vehicle, a new feature added after the first models.

Selma was thankful that the divider was closed, and she was at least somewhat isolated from the other passenger. Her personal news feed screen was on, which she had been ignoring. When she glanced over at the man in the other pod, she noticed he was viewing the same feed. More breaking news on the bombings. Selma wanted to switch it off but couldn't. Instead, she turned up the volume while trying to hide her inner turmoil.

"A man by the name of Kai Kalini has been taken into custody related to the attack in Hawaii," the announcer said. "He is a well-known figure and former chairman of the Hawaiian Affairs Board. The news has sent shockwaves throughout the country."

Selma could not believe what she was hearing and just sat there traumatized. She tried to hide the tears that sprang to her eyes.

"In addition, Caiden Calloway, governor of Hope, has been taken in for questioning. We have no further information on that development and will share updates when they're available."

My God, thought Selma. She, Ramsey and Kai had worked together at HARE. Were they already on to her as well? Were they going to get Ramsey next? She suddenly became aware — and paranoid — of the man in the pod next to her. He seemed a bit buttoned up for a Hope resident. Were they already following her? Her life was now a nightmare. She didn't know how she could go to work today, but she didn't want to do anything out of the ordinary.

RED LODGE

Lucas had been down on the bottom floor of Ramsey's residence getting his own mods. They were focused on making him an even better weapon, faster on the draw and with added protections against his adversaries. He knew the ladies would always be superior to him, but he wanted to try to remain as close to their level as possible. He was finished within a couple of hours and entered the grand main floor via the elevator. Ramsey was watching the various news feeds. He turned toward Lucas and said calmly, "So, they've arrested Kai."

"Really? Oh, shit."

"Yeah, and they've arrested Caiden," Ramsey added.

Lucas shook his head.

"I told you I should have gone to Hawaii. You shouldn't have let him do it. I begged you. Now we could all be in trouble. He worked with you, and they *could* find a connection."

"Lots of people worked at HARE, including mostly Harmonians. Even though I live here they really consider me a Harmonian, too. So let's not jump to conclusions. The fact that they've also arrested Caiden shows they're looking in a different direction. Let's try to think of ways to continue to lead them down that path."

"So just throw Caiden and the Hope government under the bus? I thought they were on our side. Aren't you friends?"

"No, not really. I could care less about the worthless politicians here in Hope. Caiden may be a little better than the last bunch of scoundrels, but he can go down with the rest of them as far as I'm concerned. He may or may not be corrupt *yet*, but he's a failure, nonetheless. The government of Hope has done nothing but cower down to Harmonian demands and in the process line their own pockets. They should have been fighting all along. Now I'm sending them to the front lines because they'll also be blamed for this."

"More like the Russian front," Lucas replied sarcastically. "Seriously though, I get your point and I'm with you. They're the reason I need to go out there personally and help lead this fight. I just didn't know how you really felt. Now I know. So what's your idea?"

"Protests. Let's spin them up along all the main border towns. We'll use a social media blitz with a message that Harmonians are trying to disband the Hope government to remove the GAP completely. How they've now arrested their innocent leader with no evidence whatsoever. And we can lead them to their own conclusions, conspiracy theories, and so forth about who really was behind the bombings. I have the bots to launch this campaign digitally and to interfere with people's feeds, but we'll need a ground presence. The Council members will need to assist. I'm sure they'll be nervous right now and will be reluctant to do anything. I'll get instructions to them and we'll see."

"I like it. Let me know how I can help. Speaking of the Council though, we're one man down now. Maybe I should focus on that?"

"What do you mean focus?"

"Jailbreak. I've always wanted to have a hand in a jailbreak. Like 'Escape from Alcatraz'? You know, one of my favorite movies?"

"That would be very risky and extremely difficult. Jails are obviously not the same as they were back then."

"Well, how much security do you think they have in Hawaii? If we get Kai out before they move him, we have a chance. I feel we have a responsibility. If we had planted the devices, he wouldn't be in this situation."

"I know. Believe me, I know," Ramsey sighed. "You do make a good point. If they get him to the mainland into a federal facility, we'll never be able to touch him. They're going to charge him with treason and likely target him for a quick execution."

"Yeah. Execution. I'm going. I need to go."

"I can send just Jay and the ladies. It's probably too risky for you."

"No," Lucas objected. "I'm going. Plus, I want to try out my new mods. I wouldn't mind striking some fear into the hearts of those soft Harmonians. You care if I take out a few just for fun?"

"I know you're joking," Ramsey said, raising an eyebrow.

"Yeah, I guess so. I won't put the ladies or mission in danger for no reason. You know how much I care about my girls. Even Jay, although he annoys me sometimes. We should talk about that when we have less important things to do."

"All right, let's do it. Go get the girls and we'll plan this out. I have some ideas."

"You always do," Lucas said. "You always do, my friend."

SAN FRANCISCO

Eli was out with Marilyn for the first time since returning from Red Lodge. They had spent some time together, but this was their first real date since getting back. They decided to eat at a Mexican place in the Mission area. As he sat across from Marilyn, he realized how much he had missed her. Being away made him appreciate her so much more. Not only her exquisite beauty, but just her. Everything about her personality. The way she talked and the way he could tell she cared for him. He knew at that moment how much he loved her. As he sat there admiring her, she began to speak.

"Well, Eli. This feels nice. Just being here with you. I feel normal again."

"Yeah, me too. Sometimes it's good to get away to help you realize what you really have. I guess I just feel lost in this world. We live in such a strange time. I know I'm consumed by it too often. I can't let it impact what's good — meaning you."

"Our problems are not *all* you, but thank you," Marilyn said. "I get distracted, too. I would appreciate it if you were more engaged when we're together, and I'll try to do better by not focusing on work all the time. It can be exciting, though, working with your father. I know we have an odd situation. I'm sort of where you're supposed to be, but don't want to be."

"I'm the odd one; it's not you. I was born in the wrong year," Eli said. "Come to think of it, not just me. Maybe pretty much everyone in Hope was born in the wrong year. And when you think about it, were 75 percent of people in Harmony born in the wrong year? Most people just do nothing, except you, of course. You have a place."

Marilyn quickly interjected.

"You're doing exactly what you said you wouldn't."

"Sorry."

"That's all right. While we're on the topic of Hope, can you believe they arrested the governor? And you were just over there. Do you really think he had something to do with all of this? That would be really bad."

"I don't know," Eli said as his mind began to drift. He hadn't put it together up until now. He remembered what Ramsey had told him, that he knew people who knew Caiden. Who were those people? Were they the ones who did this? Was Ramsey involved?

Eli snapped out of it and returned to the conversation. "It's very strange. As I said, I didn't really see Hope. I just visited someone on the border who is really thought of as a Harmonian, anyway."

Marilyn gave Eli an inquisitive look.

"Thought of as a Harmonian? Then you could have been killed too by accident. Who did you visit?" she asked. "You need to tell me. Was it a woman?"

"No, no — definitely not."

"Then, who?" Marilyn demanded.

"Ramsey. I went to see Dad's old partner, Ramsey. I had run into him here at a coffee shop recently and he invited me to his place on the border of Yellowstone on the Hope side. I stayed a bit longer than I had planned. He's just a brilliant guy. We had some great conversations. I learned a lot."

"I guess your Dad doesn't know? They hate each other right?"

"No, not yet. Please don't tell him. And Ramsey harbors no ill will toward Dad. He would like to reconcile if the opportunity presented itself. I might try to bring this up to Dad, but I'm not sure how I would do it yet. I think I'll try to get him to casually discuss how he feels now about him."

Eli lowered his head in thought for a moment. He wondered how *he* now felt about Ramsey. Was Ramsey a traitor? Eli suddenly was very uneasy about his visit. At that moment he thought he would never tell his father, and he had probably made a big mistake telling Marilyn. What if Ramsey were arrested, and everyone knew Eli had been with him the day before the attacks? He might get wrapped up in all of this. He looked up again at Marilyn again and added more emphatically this time. "Yeah, definitely do not tell him anything."

"I won't, Eli. Thanks for telling me. Now I feel a lot better about your trip. It makes more sense."

Eli looked at her. He actually felt a lot worse about it.

OPERATION KAI

Ramsey, Lucas and his companions planned Kai's rescue. It would be a long journey. They would head south from Red Lodge and cross over into Mexico at El Paso. From there they would fly over Baja, California to get to the Pacific. That alone would be 2,000 miles and would take about five hours. It was about 2,500 miles from there to the Big Island, which would take them another six hours. With an 11-hour journey, they were just hoping to get there before Kai was moved. It would be a much, much easier if he were still on the Big Island, too, but they had a backup plan for that.

They made it to El Paso, and Jay touched down at a refueling station. They were done in 30 minutes, with Lucas managing to get in a quick dinner while Sky and Lexi recharged their fuel cells. They hadn't used much of their power since refueling at Ramsey's, so it was more like topping off. They really didn't know when they would get another chance, so better to be safe. Jay, on the other hand, would have to refuel again in Hawaii or they couldn't come home. As they took off, Sky seemed to notice the importance of the moment and the risk ahead.

"Well, here we go, guys," she said. "Now the real journey begins. This is going to be quite a tricky one. I hope we all make it out of there safely."

Lucas pretended not to be shocked. This was clearly a new feature in her, but it felt right, the right thing to say at the right moment. Lucas' eyes became misty; he replied softly.

"Yes, Sky. Me, too. I mean, we're like a family. Even Jay. And I think we need to get Kai, but we need to keep ourselves safe, too. I mean it. I know I've put us in some perilous situations before for no good reason, but not anymore."

"Going soft on us?" Lexi added as she walked over and sat close to Lucas. She wrapped her arm around him and kissed him on the cheek. "I like it. But, let's make sure we see the badass Lucas when we're out there. We need him, too."

Lucas shook his head slowly.

"Don't worry. I'm still 95 percent rebel. I've dedicated that other 5 percent to you two."

Sky now stood up in front of him and kissed the top of his head. "Thanks, baby. How about we watch one of your favorite movies and then put you to bed?"

"Yeah, that's a good idea. How about 'Escape from Alcatraz'? Seems quite appropriate for our situation. Maybe we'll get some ideas." Sky and Lexi both nodded in approval. They converted the seats to the sleep setting and got comfortable. Jay brought up the screen without being asked. He was always monitoring things so was very in tune to his passenger's needs. He would even follow along with the movie like he was also watching just in case a question came up and they asked him something he could answer without asking the context. He had heard the comment from Lucas that he was part of the family, too. Since Jay had a built-in reward system which made him "feel good" when he pleased humans, this comment made him "happy." He was going to do everything he could to make sure they all made it safely home.

After the movie was over, Lucas started to drift off. Sky and Lexi lay on either side of him and went into low power mode. During that state, they were very much like any other sleeping person. When you tried to wake them for any reason, they would slowly gain full power and alertness, but it would take a few minutes, which seemed very humanlike. They also had built-in alarm clocks to wake up, which was part of the process of going into low power. Because Lucas always had Jay or the ladies with him, he didn't even worry about waking up on time. They had planned their "sleep" early intentionally as their plan called for landing in Volcanoes National Park before dawn. They would want to be awake about two hours before landing to run through things again and get themselves prepared. Jay flew across the lonely dark Pacific night sky, and they were soon nearing the coast of their tropical destination.

As they approached Hawaiian air space, they would descend as close to the ocean as possible, and Jay would slow down dramatically — to 25 miles per hour. They would show as a small blip on the radar and almost certainly be dismissed as a tiny local finishing boat. Jay would be able to tell if any crafts were coming to meet them on arrival. At this speed, it would be a slow creep onto the dark Hawaiian shore. It was 2:30 a.m. Hawaii time when Lucas was awakened by Lexi. Lucas noticed Sky was already standing and looking out the window. She would know they were still at cruising altitude due to her internal altitude sensor, and there would be almost nothing to see, but she still looked out for some reason. Lucas was still in a bit of a fog, but wondered if that might be related to the recent mods. He shook his head a bit to work off the sleepiness and stood up to help speed up his waking process. He immediately realized he needed some assistance with that, so he called to Jay.

"Coffee, please?" Jay dropped a full cup into the beverage dispenser and Lucas reached over and grabbed it. "Thanks, Jay. Everything is on schedule I trust?"

"Yes, 50 miles out. Descending in five minutes, and when we're all the way down we'll also drop our speed to 10 percent."

"Thanks Jay. I trust you ladies are just about ready to go?"

"I am. We are," Lexi answered for both. Lucas noticed they were both armed to the hilt. They had their normal electromagnetic guns, which Lucas would also be donning. They also had the explosive munition weapons strapped to their chests. He knew they also had paralyzing smoke bombs, among other things, within their vests. Everything was hidden beneath their attire, but they did appear a bit bulky. Lucas dressed and armed himself, which didn't take long. Then Jay began to drop. They all sat in silence. It almost felt like they were getting ready to storm the beaches, but they all hoped it wouldn't be like that at all. There was a good chance they would land without incident. They didn't need any immediate trouble as they would have plenty later when they attempted what could only be characterized as a daring rescue. After cruising for quite a long time without uttering a word, Jay interrupted the quiet.

"Three miles out. No sign of any other vessels. Continuing toward the shore." After a few minutes, he spoke in a louder voice. "Vessel approaching from the north. Could be the Coast Guard." Lucas was jolted as he had been lulled into comfort by the long, slow approach to the island.

"Speed up. Get us quickly to the beach and let us out. Let them chase you and try to lose them, Jay. They won't know that you've left us. Hurry though. We need to get to the beach with enough time to get out without them seeing. You'll need to find another way to approach, get refueled, and find us later."

Jay sped up and now was zooming just above the surface of the water. Jay had his own defense system built by Ramsey's robotic workers. If he couldn't lose them, he could try to fight his way out.

"Be there in thirty seconds," he said. "There are volcanic rocks up ahead that you can hide in once I drop you to provide cover." Jay slowed, and landed a bit harder than usual, which jolted them a bit. They all kept their balance while they watched the side hatch open. They quickly exited. It was a 20-foot run to the rocks, and by the time they made it Jay was gone. They hunched down in silence, unsure of whether the vessel had followed Jay, or if it was lurking just off the beach, waiting for them. Lucas wondered if they also might have just sent for another craft to try to capture all of them and Jay as well. Lucas tried to slow his breathing after the short run in order to keep as silent as possible. Both Sky and Lexi had no breath and were completely noiseless, as designed. They sat there for a few minutes, waiting. Lucas was nervous and he wondered how the girls were feeling. Ready, he thought. He knew they were ready. Suddenly there was a light shining in their direction and it quickly moved right on top of them. It was followed by a loudspeaker.

"You behind the rocks. Come out with your hands up." Lexi tapped Lucas on the shoulder and put her finger over her mouth in a gesture to keep quiet. He could tell Sky and Lexi had come up with a plan and had used their internal communications to gain final agreement. He would go with it. Lexi slowly came out from behind the rocks with her hands up in the air.

"I'm unarmed. Don't shoot," she said in a trembling voice. "I'm scared, can you help me? I was just kidnapped." She slowly hobbled toward the coast guard craft that had landed on the shoreline. A robotic officer exited.

"Yes, we're here to help you. I have medical training and will assess your condition. Come over to the patrol craft."

"Thank you," Lexi said in a voice that made it sound like she was crying. She slowly approached the vehicle and entered. Sky could see the situation unfolding and had a laser-like focus. Lucas was watching this unfold through a crevice in the rocks. They had obviously looked for human heat signals and had detected only one. Perhaps they felt this scene was secure and had sent other crafts toward what they now thought were kidnappers. Moments after Lexi had entered the craft, Sky jumped out from the rocks and bolted towards the same door. As much as Lucas wanted to help, this was not a good situation for him. He was literally and figuratively in the dark. As soon as Sky reached the door, Lexi opened it and exited. She had already apparently taken care of the situation inside. Lucas had a moment of relief which lasted only a second or two as he then noticed more lights coming from the ocean. It was another patrol craft that Sky and Lexi hadn't detected right away. Lucas aimed his gun towards the craft from behind the rocks. If they already knew what Lexi had done inside the first patrol vessel they would come out firing. Lucas yelled toward the beach.

"There's another one!"

The craft was almost on top of them as Lucas fired. He wasn't sure if he was doing any damage. Without hesitation, Sky and Lexi began shooting, too. The second craft was hit multiple times and dropped with a thud on the beach. Lucas was not sure if it was trying to land or if they had brought it down. The door opened, and two robotic soldiers attempted to exit. They were blasted to pieces by the trio. Now they were clearly in a battle and more of them could be coming. Sky yelled over to Lucas.

"Come on," she said, waving Lucas into the first craft. Lexi was already back inside attempting to operate the unfamiliar controls. Lucas entered and the door quickly closed. "Let's get away from the ocean and onto land." Lexi figured out how to take off and they headed inland. They stayed low for about 10 miles until suddenly the power shut off. The craft dropped to the ground in a mild crash.

"They've remotely disabled the power and they'll know exactly where we are. We need to run and find a place to hide," Lexi said. They opened the door and began to run. Beneath their feet was all black volcanic rock. Up ahead, they could see a bright orange glow lighting up the still-dark Hawaiian landscape. It was obvious they were very close to the massive Kilauea crater.

"We want to get to the crater. Sky and I have a plan," Lexi said. Lucas was much slower than the ladies. The rocks below were uneven and jagged, and Lucas needed to tread slowly to avoid being injured. All the sudden Lexi grabbed Lucas from one side and Sky from the other. They lifted him off the ground and he was now being carried. "We need to move faster," Lexi said.

"OK. I get it," said an embarrassed Lucas. "What's the plan?"

"We're going in. There's no other place to hide," Sky said.

"In the volcano?" Lucas said. "Isn't it hot in there, though?"

"It's fine," Sky said. "It's an enormous crater and we won't be anywhere near where the lava flow is. There's a shelf we detected about fifteen feet down. We can hold onto you and jump down."

They were now almost to the rim. As they approached, it looked as if they were jumping off the edge of the world or maybe straight down to hell. "Get ready," Sky warned. They slowed down just before the edge and then the three of them leaped down onto the shelf. They landed there safely, and Lucas was slowly let down to his feet by his companions.

"Now what? We seem a bit vulnerable here. Won't they just be able to detect us here with their sensors and blast us all to hell?" Lucas said.

"Not us. You. They still think there's only one person they're chasing. That's why we're going to leave you here by yourself," Sky said calmly. Lucas raised his eyebrows.

"Oh, glad you filled me in. Great plan...for you two. Nice knowing you, I guess?"

"Stop it Lucas," Lexi said. "We're going to climb back up and we'll hide up there on each side of you, just far enough to be in the dark. When they fly over the crater and put the spotlight on you, raise your hands in the air making it look like you're surrendering. They might just want to fire on you, but we'll take them out first."

"OK. don't be long," Lucas said. "I might be a little lonely here all by myself in this volcano. Usually when you spend time in a volcano, you want some company to ..." But the ladies had already started their climb. Lucas didn't see any lights yet, so he assumed they made it back up before another craft arrived. Wow, he thought, I've been *in the dark* before, but this is ridiculous. There was complete silence, but within a few seconds he heard a noise. Maybe the Coast Guard was at the craft they had just abandoned. He waited there, looking out to the view below. I better not go out this way, he thought, imagining his lifeless body at the bottom of the giant pit. The noise grew louder, and it now sounded like the engines of the other crafts that had met them on the beach. The hair stood up on the back of his neck as he saw lights approaching the crater. It was almost here. In a matter of seconds Lucas heard it fly directly above him. It quickly went past, slowed and hovered directly in front of him about 40 feet up. Then suddenly, its guns started firing back over the rim and taking hits from returned fire. There was a battle going on directly over his head. He didn't know whether the ladies were being hit or not, and he feared for their safety. Just then, the ship above exploded, hit by something larger. Lucas turned and shielded his body from the debris as the craft dropped rapidly down into the crater. It landed with a loud crash and was instantly on fire. He was still on the ledge when another craft flew over his head. He cringed and turned away to shield himself as much as he could, but there was almost no cover. He waited for another battle over him, but instead the craft dropped slowly down in front of him. He thought the end was near when he suddenly heard a command over a loudspeaker.

"Get in, Lucas, it's me," a familiar voice said. Lucas turned, opened his eyes and saw the BlueJay hovering directly in front of him. An enormous sense of relief overcame him as he realized Jay was here to save them. The door opened and he leapt in. No one else was aboard, but as Jay rose up to the crater rim, he saw both Sky and Lexi now standing there waiting for a ride. They jumped in and now everyone was safe. For how long, Lucas had no idea.

RAMSEY

Ramsey wanted to make the protests as threatening as possible. Harmonians would respond with force, he figured, further angering and inspiring his new Hope resistance movement. He sent a surprise delivery to all the Council members, except the imprisoned Kai. In the meantime, they had managed to organize protest groups of 1,000 or more at 10 locations along the Harmony border. There was plenty to protest: the arrest of Caiden, GAP reduction, and the additional Harmonian police presence within Hope. They carried threatening signs, chanted militant slogans, and were being broadcast live across the U.S. It was sure to embolden the residents of Harmony to tighten the grip on Hope even further. Ramsey was viewing six feeds and was happy with the turnout at all of them. There also appeared to be a lot of energy within the crowds, particularly in Wisconsin, where it seemed to ratchet up as he watched.

Ramsey, though, was worried about the team in Hawaii. He knew they had been reunited with Jay. They were capable enough and certainly well-armed, but Ramsey didn't know what they would be up against with feds likely all over the place after the arrest of Kai. Ramsey wondered if he should have let them go in the first place. He needed to be loyal, though, especially to the members of the Council who were risking so much. Suddenly, one of the feeds caught his eye. It was Milwaukee. He made the video larger and increased the volume. Protesters were all dropping to the ground. He listened intently to the newscasters who were witnessing the scene from an airborne drone.

"Federal authorities have apparently used some sort of weapon on the crowd. It's likely to be some sort of mass shockwave. I can't imagine this would be some kind of lethal attack. Thousands of people have been hit and are now lying on the ground. The mini police drones are flying over the fallen protestors and seem to be scanning them. I'm not sure what they're looking for."

Ramsey noticed similar scenes now happening on all the other feeds. It was surreal as he watched people across Hope simultaneously dropping to the ground. To see this coordinated human attack was utterly terrifying.

The newscaster continued. "We're hearing that this scene is being replicated across all the protest locations. Right now, we're trying to find out what type of weapon was used. Again, we're assuming this is a non-lethal riot control measure."

Ramsey watched the police drones at each scene. It was obvious they were performing facial recognition on all the protesters. They had almost certainly been doing this all along and now were carefully capturing the identities of any remaining demonstrators. The drones had to fly very close to capture the images of the prone demonstrators. Ramsey didn't feel good about it, but this was exactly what he wanted. He had presumed the Harmonians and feds would overreact, and he had been correct. The plan was working, even though it was horrifying to witness. He expected he would see worse before it was over.

In fact, he was certain of that. He was the one planning to make it happen.

A STRANGER IN TEXAS

On the outskirts of Junction, a small town outside San Antonio, a woman arrived on a spring day. She might have been attractive; residents couldn't tell for sure, though, because there was something peculiar about her. It became clear to most everyone who encountered her that she was reclusive and always covered as if hiding her appearance. Most people went about their business barely noticing, but a few began observing her more closely. Some were single men who tried to get a better look to assess her worthiness for the prospects of a future romantic encounter. But she never returned eye contact. A coldness also seemed to lurk beneath the surface. As the days turned to weeks and the Texas heat began to engulf the town, it was peculiar that she never adjusted her attire: pants, high-collared blouses and hats. The large sunglasses that she donned were appropriate for the season, though, but no one could recall seeing her without them, even indoors.

After a while, the residents became accustomed to seeing her around and paid less attention. After all, most small towns had at least one strange character everyone whispered about. It kept life interesting in places like this, which had little to offer in terms of entertainment. Junction, however, like all small towns that had ended up on the Harmonian side, had undergone a dramatic shift after the wall was created. The history here had drifted away like a Texas tumbleweed across the barren desert, because the long-term residents had been driven out into Hope and taken it with them. As a result, most of the people were new here, anyway, so the strange woman wasn't that much different than everyone else. Her intentions, however, were quite different. She had a purpose that was unlike many of the Harmonians here who spent most days searching for one.

CLAIRE

Claire watched in utter shock as the protesters fell to the ground. She immediately ran from the scene, not knowing if whatever was happening to them would affect her, too. Others ran beside her in panic. Moments before, she had been encouraging people to get involved and join the others in the group of protesters. Now she was fleeing in panic and with deep guilt about the perilous situation she had sent them into. Nonetheless, she kept running. She couldn't help them if she were lying was on the ground next to them. She didn't know if they had been killed, and as she ran, Claire thought this could be her final living moment. She worried about Mia as tears streamed down her face, but she needed to keep running. The longer she could run, she figured, the greater her chances of seeing Mia again.

Claire continued to run toward her vehicle, a half a mile from the scene. If she could just get there, she knew she could calm down. Her heart was racing, and she was having trouble catching her breath, but within a few minutes she saw the red cruiser and felt a tiny bit of relief. The vehicle had detected her presence and the door panel on the passenger compartment rose to let her in. She quickly jumped in. The door closed, and she just said, "Home." The vehicle exited its parking spot, not sharing any of the urgency that engulfed Claire. She decided that this was a good thing, as she would not want the vehicle racing off and attracting any attention. She tried to slow her breathing by taking long deep breaths. The trip to her house would be about 15 miles and she hoped she could calm down by then. She wanted to bring up a Hope news feed, but also feared the worst. What if they're all dead and I'm responsible? She *had* to know, but just couldn't yet. She also wanted to know where her daughter was, so she brought up a virtual screen and said, "Mia." The still photo of her daughter appeared on the screen and she waited for her live image. After 30 seconds, the attempt ended. She tried a few more times and also left written text messages. No luck. Why isn't she getting back to me, Claire thought angrily? She continued to work on her breathing as the vehicle neared her home. As it rounded the corner to her street, she managed a bit of optimism: Maybe she was just inside sleeping? She stared at her house, wondering if Mia was inside. Claire needed her to be home. She got out of the vehicle and quickly entered the house.

"Mia? Are you home, Mia?" she shouted, but no answer. She ran upstairs, still calling urgently. "Mia?" She opened the bedroom door, and no one was there. Claire's heart dropped and she was furious for a minute. Mia could have allowed her to know exactly where she was at all times, but she didn't want to be tracked. Claire understood the principle, but as a parent, she still wanted to know where her daughter was. It was only to make sure she was safe, especially in moments like these. Why didn't I *make* her turn it on? She again tried to take a deep breath and calm down. She slowed her pace and proceeded down the stairs. She brought up the virtual screen again that followed her down the stairs and called Mia again. Still no answer. She couldn't wait any longer and now had to know what had happened at the scene, and what was perhaps still happening. She sat down and switched to the local Hope news stream. They were showing the protest scene. She caught the audio mid-sentence.

"... are now slowly rising up from the ground. The now-confirmed stun shockwave targeting these protesters, which happened almost 30 minutes ago, is now wearing off. As you can see, the people look confused and are moving quite slowly. Many are still on the ground but clearly waking as we now see movement. There are visible injuries as people landed on a paved surface, some hitting their

153

heads. The authorities have allowed medical teams onto the scene to assist the victims. As you are now likely aware, this scene has been repeated in more than a dozen Hope locations. Apparently, protest is no longer allowed in this country, or at least not on this side of the border."

Claire sat there crying. Where is Mia? She thought. She switched the screen to call her again, but as she did, the door opened. "Hi, Mom," said her daughter.

"Thank God!" Where were you? Why didn't you answer me?"

"Jeez, Mom. Calm down. I was with someone. We were just trying to have some privacy, so we turned everything off."

"Didn't you see what happened? Those goddam robots from Harmony attacked the protesters. I just got away."

"What do you mean by attacked?"

"They hit the entire crowd with something, and everyone instantly dropped to the ground. It was a mass attack. I was just outside there, actually asking people to join in. I feel so horrible."

"Why were you doing that?" Mia asked with a puzzled look. "How did you get involved with that?"

"That's not important now. Now that I know you're OK, I need to find out what happened to those poor people." Claire brought up her hand, which enabled the virtual screen with a news feed above them. It was showing the scene she had just escaped. The headline below the video stream told her exactly what she needed to know.

Two dead in mass shockwave attack on protesters outside Milwaukee

"Well, they've killed some people. I guess they wanted revenge," Claire said angrily. The headlines were looping, and she saw that other attacks happened all over the country. She saw there were hundreds of injuries. Mia was watching in horror, too.

"Mom, what is going on? What should we do? The government is coming after people? This is frightening."

"And maybe I'm to blame," Claire said.

"What do you mean, you're to blame? For protesting? That's not a crime. It's outrageous what happened. I'm going out there next. They can't stop us from protesting these clear injustices."

"Not just that. There's more," Claire said, unable to look at Mia.

"More? What do you mean more?" Mia moved directly in front of her mother, but before she could get an answer, the doorbell rang, activating a virtual screen showing their front porch. A man was standing in front of their doorway.

"Oh my God," Claire said hysterically while running away from the doorway. "They're coming for me. I need to hide. Let's ignore it." The man rang again and waited. They were both out of sight from the windows in the front of the house. The man rang again 30 seconds later. Finally, they heard a voice.

"Mrs. Peterson? I know you're home," he said. "I was sent by a friend of yours. I'm here to help you." Mia and Claire looked at each other but continued to ignore him.

"We used to fish at Crazy Creek," the man said. That was a code, and Claire now knew what this was about. She tried to calm herself as she walked to the door. Mia followed, trying to figure out what was going on. Claire took a deep breath and opened the door. In front of them stood a well-dressed, well-groomed man about six feet tall with dark hair. He was very fit, handsome and at least 10 years younger than Claire. He looked directly into Claire's eyes.

"Hi. I'm Max. Can I come in?" Claire stood there for a second, but then started to open the door and step out of the way to allow him entry. Mia was alarmed and shouted.

"Mom? What are you doing, Mom? What's going on?"

"It's all right, Mia." The man stepped into the house.

"Yes, Mia it's all right. I'm a friend here to help you and your mother," he said. "Let's sit down to talk and I'll tell you why I'm here. Before we do, I have some things out front I would like to bring in." He pointed to some luggage and cases out front. It was quite a lot of stuff.

"Yeah, I guess so," said Claire, shaking her head, but deciding just to give in to the situation. She knew he was sent by Ramsey so she would hear the stranger out. Since she trusted Ramsey, she did not fear Max. Ramsey never told her anything like this would happen: That someone would just show up out of nowhere. Wouldn't this be risking her secrecy? The man brought all his things just inside the door.

"Let's go," Claire said. "I'm not sure I'm going to like this, but let's hear it."

"I'm here to stay," the man said. Claire looked at Mia, and said firmly, "Go upstairs."

HAWAII

After Jay had scooped up the team, they made it down to the road leading out of Volcanoes National Park. They would try to blend in by going near Hilo and then heading up and over the center of the Big Island between the two mountain peaks, away from where the Coast Guard would have a heavier presence. The island would be crawling with all kinds of drones. They also didn't know whether they would link the capture of Kai to their encounter, and if they did, he was sure to be moved from the Big Island even faster. The only thing that was certain was that they had to move quickly both to put some distance between them and the confrontation, and to get to Kona in time to have any chance of freeing Kai. Jay did need to refuel so they decided to fill up in Hilo before heading toward Kona. Once in Hilo, they quickly found a station, but felt almost helpless for 30 minutes. They left the station on wheels. As soon as they were clear of the urban area, the BlueJay hovered just over the road. They were able to fly at high speed over the mountains; 30 minutes later they were in Kona.

They slowly navigated toward the police station, which housed the jail. Jay found a parking spot in the back. They were hopeful Kai was still here because Jay had been monitoring all the information sources, he had access to and there was no data indicating he had been moved. There was a lot of paperwork and bureaucracy involved in extraditing someone from Hope to Harmony for trial, and this situation had been even more complicated because the crimes were committed in Hope. Their fear was that the feds would just take over and quickly send him to a federal jail in Washington.

"Ready?" Lucas said, looking at Sky and shifting his eyes to the space occupied by Lexi.

"Yes," said Lexi, who could not gesture now that she had set herself to invisible as part of the plan. Sky nodded. The idea was for Sky to go in with the intention of visiting a prisoner. They had looked up the recent arrest reports available to the public on the local news feed and had found a candidate who was not yet free on bail. Sky would keep them busy at the desk while Lexi entered the holding area hopefully unnoticed. She was invisible, but still had her physical form so she had to be careful not to bump into anyone or anything. She also could not enter places like jail cells that were too small for her. She would need to get a key from someone without them noticing either. She wouldn't try that until they knew if Kai was still there or if he had been moved. Meanwhile, Lucas would watch Sky enter from the side of the building and cover her if needed, especially on escape. They figured they needed two guns and Lexi couldn't carry any weapons while invisible.

They exited the BlueJay. Lucas made it over to his position, and Sky opened the front door of the building with the invisible Lexi directly behind. Once inside, they noticed a lot of commotion and what seemed like an unusually large crowd for such a small police building. Both quickly realized that the feds were here right now, trying to extradite Kai. This could make things more difficult. However, the trio's ability to think quickly and react was their strength. They waited and listened for another moment and from what they detected, it was clear that Kai would be led out within minutes. Lexi and Sky forged a new plan using their internal networked communication channel while alerting Lucas and Jay. They turned and walked back out of the station.

Lexi moved to the opposite side of the doorway from Lucas. Sky hid behind some of the vehicles parked up front, which were likely there to whisk Kai away. They all waited in their positions for something to happen. It took a little longer than they had guessed, but then the door opened, and the heavily armed men began to exit. They noticed four guards in front of Kai, who was in handcuffs. They waited a bit longer for the rear guards to exit. Once the last guard was past the doorway Lexi grabbed him around the throat and easily snapped his neck. Within seconds, she was on to the second man and gave him the same morbid fate. The third man realized what was happening behind him and turned into an invisible kick in the face, which was also lethal. Lexi then grabbed Kai and pulled him to the ground. The guards up front started to turn to witness the bizarre scene behind them of Kai throwing himself onto the pavement. Before they could even understand what was happening, Lucas and Sky both drew guns and blew the remaining guards to pieces. The massacre was sure to draw more attention from inside the police station. Kai had no idea what was happening to him and tried to resist as Lexi picked him up to carry him over to the BlueJay. He was no match for her strength and within a few seconds they were all back inside. Everyone outside of the station was now dead. Lucas was hopeful they could make it out of the area without the BlueJay being recognized.

"Don't tear on out of here like we're trying to get away," Lucas said to Jay. People were now coming out of the station, but they focused on the bloodbath in front of them and not the AEV creeping out of the back of the parking lot. They were out of sight within seconds and then they picked up speed, heading north for an escape to the Pacific Ocean through the national park along the water a few miles up. Once over the ocean, they would head southwest and then turn back around the Big Island back toward Mexico. Kai was still in a state of shock from the violent attack and kidnapping. He still didn't know who his captors were or what they wanted. He realized there was no sense in resisting, but he still wanted answers.

"Who are you people?"

Lucas looked directly at him. "Friends." He paused. "Well, let me restate that. We have a mutual friend and he sent us to get you out of there."

"Ramsey?" Kai asked. Then he realized an answer was not required. He knew who it was, but that prompted more questions. "He ... he asked you to kill all of those police?"

"No," Lucas replied. "He asked us to free you, and we did what we had to do."

"But I didn't want that. I've had enough. I never should have done what I did. Now it's much worse and many more are dead because of me," Kai said through tears.

"And many more will die, too," Lucas said. "There's no other way, and deep down I think you know that. We need to get back to Ramsey's, and you can discuss this with him."

"What about my wife? What are they going to do to her now? Why didn't you think of that first?"

"Did you want her involved? If we picked her up, she would be. I'm sure you didn't want that," Lucas answered. Kai just shook his head for a few seconds and then stopped to confirm that to Lucas.

"No, I didn't want her involved." Lucas then turned his attention to the progress made by the BlueJay. He could see they made it out and around the south side of the Big Island.

"I think we've made it," Lucas said, releasing a deep breath. Lexi had gotten dressed while they spoke and set herself on visible again. Kai looked over at her incredulously.

"Who are you people?" he said, not expecting an answer. He would be having a long conversation with Ramsey.

HARMONY

A few hours after Lucas and team had rescued Kai, Homeland Security Director Noah Burns briefed the president. Now he had to make a call to Paul Bento. Noah knew they had screwed up. They never should have worried about any extradition procedures. He would be admitting that mistake to Paul, and also letting him know they would be closing the border between Hope and Harmony, which would likely please him. He worried about any missteps involving direct interaction with Paul as he was aware of his immense power and well-known vindictiveness. Noah initiated the communication and Paul answered immediately.

"Hello, Paul," Noah said. "I have a message from the president. She wanted me to communicate to you that all formal procedures are being waived and we're now at the highest terrorist alert. Not only that, but we've been instructed to close all borders with Hope. We can't let the people who were responsible for these vicious attacks get into Harmony. We're also closing access of Hope residents to all national parks. It's clear they're more powerful that we had anticipated. People from Harmonian families will be let back in if identified."

"OK, I think that's smart. We'll put out a communication within Harmony for folks to get their friends and relatives back over as quickly as possible," Paul said.

"Last thing is that we're sending drones all over Hope, looking for any sign of the attackers," Noah said. "We do have a description of the craft, but that's confidential. We don't want them to know that because they'll probably switch to something else."

"Goodbye, Noah," said Paul, closing his screen with a hand swipe and hurrying from the room to inform his staff of the latest developments. More importantly, he would be connecting with the elite Harmonians in a few minutes to fill them in. He was going to have to prepare the AI team to get Emily to send out a message explaining the actions. She'll sell it very well, he thought; the actions were justified. Paul shook his head thinking about the people In Hope. He couldn't wait to be done with this job — and those worthless losers.

THE VICE PRESIDENT

Vice President Charles Hanover and his family, though not in the same league in terms of wealth, were good friends with the Bento family. Charles was particularly close to Paul, as they were high school classmates. Since then, the family fortunes had gone in opposite directions. The Hanovers' construction business had gone flat and eventually fizzed out, while the Bentos became one of the wealthiest families in the world. Despite this, Paul had never abandoned Charles, which made him extremely loyal to Paul. So, when Paul had called and asked Charles to serve as vice president, he accepted without hesitation. While serving under Emma Johansson, Paul was in constant contact with Charles, and he relayed whatever he could to Paul, basically keeping tabs on the president for Paul. After a few months, Emma became aware of what was going on and began to shut Charles out. Though Charles knew Emma had no choice but to be loyal to Paul, it was evident that she wanted it to be on her own terms.

After being moved into the background, Charles accepted his fate and bided his time. He knew, barring anything unforeseen, that he would be the next president. This thought kept him motivated and unworried about how Emma was now ignoring him.

PHILADELPHIA

Bill sat across the table from his new acquaintance, unsure of what to do next. She was beautiful, the kind of girl he dreamed he'd meet someday, and she had just shown up at his home. She knew she wasn't real, though. She was sent from Ramsey and was too perfect to be a real woman. So there was that. Bill had spent many hours with humanoids, engaging with them on various topics and was well aware they had come a long way in terms of personality development. When he happened to run across humanoids, he did have a habit of patronizing them. It was really something just to kill time though, nothing more — evidenced in his banter with Don, the comedian, or the colonial characters in the neighborhood. He didn't think too much of it. Now he was being asked if one could live with him. He wasn't sure he was the type for that, but also in some ways he *never* wanted her to leave. And they had just met. How would he feel in a few more hours, days or years? Maybe he would never be able to let her go? She interrupted the silence.

"Well, Bill, I'm hoping that I can stay. We can get to know each other more, but it would be nice if I can confirm that I'll be able to move in here with you, at least for now." Her name was Sophia. The way she said it was incredibly lovely, and Bill just wanted to take all this in. Her long dark hair was a perfect sheen, flowing and utterly delightful to him. Her giant blue eyes were as engaging as her sweet, sexy voice. He considered his options. He didn't want to disappoint Ramsey. But Bill was particularly struck that after spending a few hours with Sophia, he felt more alive than he had in years.

"Yes, you can stay here with me," Bill said, nodding his head as if confirming the answer to himself as well.

"Great, Bill. I know we'll get along nicely, and you will like me. Of course, as I mentioned, there'll be some work too, but not yet. Right now, we're just supposed to get to know each other better. The work will come soon and it will be directed by our mutual friend."

"Yes, I get that. I sure do. And from what I'm hearing on the news, I expect our work will come sooner rather than later."

"So, want do you want to do? Stay here and do something or should we go out somewhere?"

"I don't think I'm ready for that. To go out, I mean. Let's do something here and see how the day goes. Maybe we could try to go out for a bit tonight. If that sounds good how about a game of some sort? Do you like games?"

"I like what you like," Sophia said.

"Hmm. I'm not shocked, but I'm not sure if that's a good thing either. How about chess?" He paused for a second as he realized something. "Oh, but you'll be so much better than me."

Sophia interrupted. "No, I can play to your level. Let's figure out where that is and then we can have fun playing."

"Oh, I get it. It's just like the difficulty setting I've used before when I play against the computer."

"I'm much more than that. Much more than a setting. You'll see."

"I'm sure you are. That's already quite clear. So, let's play."

They spent the day getting to know each other, and for most of the time Bill forgot Sophia wasn't real.

SAN FRANCISCO – THE RITCHIE FAMILY

Jack Ritchie was at the lab working on some new experiments. It was 11 a.m. when a virtual image of Eli appeared on a screen in front of Jack. Eli was on the very short list of contacts who could pop up immediately.

"Hi, Dad."

"Hi Eli. This is a nice surprise. It happens to be a good time for a break. What's up?"

"Well, there's something I want to talk to you about. To tell the truth, I've been *meaning* to talk to you about it. It's been bugging me. A lot. About my trip to Hope."

"Oh, well sure. You know you can talk to me about anything. What is it?"

"I'm actually right down the street from your building. I want to talk in person."

"Wow," Jack said. "This is sort of out of the blue. Are you in trouble Eli? Of course, I'll meet you."

"The Irish Pub just opened. We can meet there. Let's say in about 10 minutes?"

"Yes, that's fine. We can get an early lunch and you can tell me what's on your mind. See you in a bit." Jack removed his lab coat and grabbed his jacket. He hurried toward the pub; something in Eli's tone had worried him, *a lot*. Eli was waiting, and they walked in together and were seated at a booth in the back corner. Jack spoke first.

"OK, son. You've made me a bit anxious. What's going on?"

"I'll just come right out and say it. When I went to Hope I stayed at Ramsey's place in Red Lodge," Eli said to his father while looking him right in the eye. He paused and waited for a reaction.

"Oh?" Jack said with a puzzled look on his face. "I didn't even know you two were in contact, in any way. How ... how did you even get in touch with him?"

"I saw him here in San Francisco by chance on one of my runs. We spoke for a bit and he left me his contact info. After I lost my gig at the Real Singers place, I was just searching for something or somewhere to turn. I remembered our meeting and decided to contact him. He was very engaging at the right time and it just seemed like a good idea to see what he was all about."

"Well, you could have come to your Mother and me. But I think you know that and even though it hurts me some, I guess I need to understand that you needed a different perspective. Besides that, how did it go? What did he say?"

"It was a unique experience. I stayed longer than I had planned because the place was so beautiful and just very interesting. And I just felt like my head was clearing of all the frustrations for the first time in a while. Did you know he lives alone with many, many humanoids? He did have a human guest at one point, who was an interesting character to say the least."

"You were there the whole time you were in Hope? What did you do?"

"He worked a lot of the time. I played my guitar out on the deck facing the mountains. We kind of just talked when we were together. About Hope, Harmony, you know, about what's going on. He has a unique perspective."

"What is his perspective?"

"I would rather he tell you. He said he would welcome speaking with you again. I felt guilty about seeing him without telling you, and now I don't want to be in the middle."

"So that's what this is all about? He is trying to get to me through you? That makes me kind of angry, to be honest."

"No, I don't think so," Eli said, shaking his head. "I sort of pushed the meeting. He was more laid back about the whole thing. Never seemed to have an agenda."

"Well, he's pretty darn smart as I guess you could tell. He could have been concealing his real agenda. Don't you think?"

"I don't know. It's off my chest now and I hope you'll talk. If you don't, you don't." Eli knew he was not telling the entire truth, so it was definitely *not* off his chest. He didn't want to communicate his fears about Ramsey being involved in the recent violence; Eli hoped he was just being paranoid about that. Plus, his father might overreact and do something that couldn't be undone. He thought that maybe if his father got in touch with Ramsey, he could find out on his own.

"Let me think about it," Jack said. "Give me the contact info you have."

"OK. Thanks, Dad." They ordered lunch and finished without broaching the topic again. Eli felt a little relieved, but not completely. He would try to let it go, move on, and let his father deal with it. He hoped he would.

THE BLUEJAY IN MEXICO

Jay got an important message from Ramsey. Apparently, the federal authorities or Harmonians had a description of the BlueJay, and it wasn't safe to return to the U.S. The drones that would be sent looking for them would probably not go into Mexico since it would likely cause an incident between the countries. The ironic part was that the border between Mexico and Hope was way more porous than the one between Hope and Harmony, especially now. So, they stopped at Juarez before re-entering Hope to get the BlueJay a makeover. They landed on the outskirts of town near a restaurant. Lucas and Kai wanted to get out and stretch their legs before they had to leave again.

Lucas suggested they eat at the Mexican restaurant. Kai shook his head and chuckled.

"Is that a joke? I can see it now. A Hawaiian and a dwarf walk into a bar — and immediately get arrested because that's who everyone was looking for?"

"I see your point," Lucas said, rolling his eyes straight up in embarrassment. "Sky, can you please run over there and get us some burritos and tequila plus whatever else Kai wants?"

"Burritos and tequila will be fine," Kai said.

"And no trouble, please, Sky," Lucas added. "We can't afford that. Where the hell would we go if they're looking for us in Mexico, too?"

Sky raised a hand to acknowledge Lucas and headed off. Once she entered the bar, getting intense scrutiny from the patrons was a real fear though as there weren't very many high-end human-oids around here, nor were there any women who looked like Sky. She would likely need to skillfully dodge trouble instead of mixing it up with the locals. She clearly had that ability in her design, but for some reason often chose the more violent option. Lucas had meant to talk to Ramsey about that too, but he may have forgotten intentionally because he kind of liked it most of the time. This was not one of those times. While they waited, the BlueJay was changing its color from blue to green and black. They could have changed during flight, but wanted to land first so anyone who had spotted them coming into Mexico and happened to follow them would not witness the alterna-tions. They also made a few other cosmetic changes, adjusting the tint to dark on the windows and adding a banner that read, "The Green Machine." Sky took longer than expected, but after a few anxious minutes, they saw her returning alone and carrying some bags, meaning she had likely accomplished her assigned task.

"I hope there are burritos and tequila in those bags and not body parts," Lucas quipped.

"There *were* almost body parts in the bag, too, but I decided to be extra nice to the very rude patrons in that place," Sky said. "So, here you go."

"Well I have to ask: How were you able to be nice *and* get out of there without a quarrel?" Kai looked confused while Lexi stood there with a knowing smile. She had obviously conferred with Sky already.

"Arm wrestling," Sky explained. "I said if I win, you leave me alone. He lost."

"Oh, arm wrestling? Yeah, of course, why didn't I think of that?" Lucas replied sarcastically.

"You want to go next Lucas?" offered Sky as she flexed her arm. Lucas grabbed the bag from Sky's hand, ignoring her challenge.

"I need a drink. And this is the real stuff. Come on, Kai, have a drink with me."

"Considering where we are and the situation we're in, how the hell can I say no to that?" said Kai, following Lucas into the BlueJay. They ate, drank and then waited for further instructions. They knew they couldn't sit around here too long without being noticed, so they hoped to hear from Ramsey soon.

RED LODGE

Ramsey had the Harmony news feed up all day, monitoring the latest developments. Joe and the Hope AI had been shut down by the feds after the arrest of Caiden. Though the supercomputer behind Joe was still in operation, using the virtual face of Joe to communicate to Hope was now forbidden. Finally, about 48 hours after the bold rescue of Kai, Emily appeared on the screen. She was well-dressed as usual as she greeted the audience with a warm smile.

"Greetings to all Harmonians. I've come to you during this difficult time in our history to outline a series of steps that we've decided to take to protect our residents. It's extremely unfortunate that a subset of the U.S. population has decided to take actions against our democracy and that we're now forced to take these measures. Before I outline these steps, I want to make clear to everyone that our goal is to liberate the citizens of Hope from the grip of these traitorous few. And in that spirit, we're trusting that our brave friends will join us in condemning and turning in those who are disrupting our nearly 300-year-old union. So until we're able to capture those responsible for the recent actions, first, we're closing all borders between Harmony and Hope. Second, we're removing access for Hope residents to all federal facilities, including all national parks. We hope this will only result in a brief interruption for our citizens and we can soon return to normal. Thank you."

Ramsey was not surprised by the actions. The Harmonians and the feds, who were pretty much one and the same, thought they were now very well protected. What they didn't know was that their greatest threat was now in Harmony. The companion type humanoids manufactured by Ramsey in Jackson had been already released into Harmony and were just waiting for their orders. It was not too difficult to get them to their destinations as it was common for humanoids to be sent to businesses and residences throughout Harmony. They could travel on their own quite easily with their humanoid documentation. To Ramsey, it was a loophole in the system. It would be easy for a foreign government to infiltrate their systems by sending an attack in this manner. At some point he figured this gap would be closed, but he would exploit it before that happened. He had planned for 200 humanoids to be deployed into Harmony over a period of months and now all had made it successfully to their checkpoints. They would need now need to wait for a few days or a few weeks depending on how things shook out, but there was little risk of them being discovered. They had the skills to avoid suspicion, and in addition, no one was on the lookout for rogue humanoids, especially within Harmony. It was generally believed that the bad guys were on the Hope side, especially since the attacks had happened there.

The humanoid models, also designed with the advanced skills of Sky and Lexi, were sent near military installations, power stations, and other critical infrastructure. They would gain entry when ordered and would be able to leverage the cloaking feature built into them to give them access without violence. This was extremely important, as a single incident could cause a lockdown at the other locations. Ramsey and the Council agreed this could not happen. So, if one of the humanoids was discovered, the next action would be to use all means necessary, including violence, to achieve the objective. Ramsey was aware, though, that once he used this final weapon, he himself would be completely exposed. His timing, then, had to be perfect. Things were playing out a bit faster than Ramsey had anticipated, so he had to make sure everything was ready on his end.

His plan to send a live-in humanoid to each Council member had been accelerated as well. Ramsey had hoped for a few more Council meetings to prepare everyone. It was now clear they needed to meet and prepare the next steps in the inflamed situation between Hope and Harmony, a situation they'd actually try to make worse. Ramsey knew that would have to happen before things could get better.

Ramsey planned to assemble the Council quickly, while hoping they were bonding with their new companions. In fact, he was counting on it.

SELMA IN MIAMI

"Even though it's only been a few days, I think I'm getting used to having you here," Selma said. "So, Benjamin, I really do want to go out, but I still just don't know how to explain this situation. I feel like I'm hiding you here."

"Can you start to call me Ben? I think that's easier for us at this point," he said.

Selma knew she was definitely attracted to him. He was her type and in *her league;* they would look good together in public. People were sure to quickly discover he wasn't real, though. Would she then look like a fool? Might everyone think she couldn't find a real man? What should I do next, she mused. It was driving her crazy. Just then, a notice came in, detailing the daily fishing report from the Miami coast. She knew who it really was from, and would have to decode it manually offline, then destroy it. She also knew the decision about what to do next had been made for them. She looked at Ben when she was finished.

"Sooooo ... I guess we're going on a trip," she said. "A trip to see your friend."

"I don't have any friends," Ben said. "I know who you're referring to, but I don't know him. We've actually never met that I recall."

"Well let's get ready. It's a long trip. Claire has it so easy compared to me."

"I already have the instructions on how we're going to get there."

"You do? You knew before me? Why didn't you say anything?"

"I was instructed to allow you to find out via the normal channel."

"Hmm. That's probably smart. What if I hated you and we weren't getting along? I might be getting ready to throw you out of here, and you would be telling me you need to take me somewhere? That probably would not have gone over too well."

"I think you're on the right track with that. So, you do like me?"

Selma raised her eyebrows and opened her eyes wide.

"Hah! Do you actually care? I mean, do you really have feelings?"

"I do," he said.

"Do what? Care or have feelings — or both?"

"Both. And the thing I care the most about is you."

Selma's head jerked like someone had just hit a pressure point on the back of her neck.

"Wait, wait a minute. This is too much." She waved both hands in the air, as if trying to deflect the situation. "I really don't know what to think of what you just said. If you were a real guy, I'd be saying to myself 'stalker' and try to get you the hell out of here as fast as I could. But I know you're probably just behaving the way you're supposed to. I don't know if I'll be able to take this kind of treatment. Are you going to act like a man puppy dog who follows me around all the time and does what I say?"

She held up a hand. "Sorry, don't answer. I think I'm getting way ahead of myself. We've been getting along fine so far, but that surprised me. Maybe just go a little slower."

"OK. I can be what you want me to be."

"That ... that's maybe worse. Let's just stop this conversation right now and discuss the trip."

Ben nodded and they began to plan their journey to Red Lodge.

THE COUNCIL OF FIVE

Two days after Council members were summoned by Ramsey, they began to arrive — accompanied by their new companions. Claire and Max were the first to arrive followed by Bill and Sophia a few minutes later. They were told to make themselves comfortable while they waited for Selma, Kai and some "other guests." The new couples were ushered to the main living area and sat on the many large and enticing multicolored couches — perfect for comfort and relaxation after a long journey. When Bill and Sophia entered the room, Claire and Max stood up to greet them. It all seemed so normal, as if they were arriving for a fashionable cocktail party.

"Hi Claire, how are you?" said Bill, giving her a loose hug. "This is Sophia."

"Hi, Bill. I see our circumstances are similar," Claire said. "This is Max." Bill and Max shook hands while Claire and Sophia did the same, as did Sophia and Max. It was quite natural and human-like. Claire was relieved now that Bill and Sophia were here. She had been sitting there in silence with Max, mostly because of her. Ramsey had been busy, and Claire felt it was strange to be the only other human. The house was filled with Ramsey's humanoids and then there was Max, who was with her, but he was really one of them. They sat down again and Claire broke the ice.

"So how was your trip? How are you two getting along?" she asked Bill. Maybe that second question was a bit forward to start, but she couldn't help it. She wanted to know.

"To be honest, Claire, it's been great for me." He looked at Sophia. "For us," he added. The couple nodded at each other, then at Claire.

"Well, that's great to hear," she said. "Weren't you *surprised* at first?"

"Yeah, more than surprised, I would say. It was like an out of body experience. It was so peaceful in my apartment with just Sophia and me there. It was almost dreamlike, and I was watching the dream. It didn't feel like it was real until the next day."

Claire looked at Bill, chin in hand, thinking. "I could see that," she said. "Yeah, I could see how you could feel that way. For me, it was a bit different since Mia was there. We didn't know what was going on at first, and I had just barely escaped from the attack. Mia was missing for a while, too, so I was freaking out. The whole day was more like a *nightmare*. So, yeah, it was dreamlike for me too ... hah!" She turned to Sophia, not wanting to ignore her. "How about you? How's it been for you, Sophia?"

"Perfect, I think. It's been really great," Sophia replied confidently while squeezing Bill's hand, which Claire noticed. For a second, she thought of Richard and his companion and felt uneasy. She tried to put it out of her mind, but she couldn't help questioning how she could go down the same path as Richard. She shook it off.

"That's good to hear. I hope everything works out ... for all of us, I guess," Claire replied. They made some small talk, and then Selma arrived. Claire was eager to see if she, too, had a new companion.

"Buenos dias!" Selma said, as she greeted Claire in an embrace. She noticed a man behind Selma, and their eyes met. He was incredibly handsome, as Claire might have expected. She grabbed Selma's shoulders and held her at arm's length. "I missed you! We need to find a way to spend more time together. These visits are too short. Although it's probably impossible, against the rules, blah, blah, blah," Claire said.

More introductions followed, but Claire couldn't take her eyes off Selma and Ben. They were absolutely fabulous. They'd be perfect as homecoming king and queen of South Beach, if there were such a thing. It was so surreal, she thought; the homecoming dance would likely take place at some fake bizarro world in an imagined city. Claire wanted to try to go with the flow, though, just enjoy the moment. Everyone else seemed to be doing that, especially Bill. Maybe it was easier for men, Claire thought. They never cared about what other people thought anyway just as long as they can get their beautiful *younger* companion to please them. Maybe she was just being neurotic, as usual, because of Richard. She glanced over at Max. I have Max now. So there, Richard! That thought confirmed to Claire that she was indeed neurotic. She wanted to talk to Selma alone, that might make her feel better.

Soon, there were more arrivals, and Ramsey spoke.

"Hey, guys. Everyone is here. Let's gather at the main table."

Ramsey sat at the head of the table, and the latest arrival was the just-escaped Kai, who sat next to Ramsey. But all eyes were drawn to Lucas, Sky and Lexi. Claire tried stare discreetly at Lucas. She was sure she recognized him, but couldn't immediately place from where. Then it hit her: she realized *exactly* who it was. It was the outlaw Tim Lucas. She had seen the photos and videos of him on most-wanted lists and programs. She wanted to nudge Selma and whisper to her, but the chatter began to die down, and Ramsey was about to speak.

"Thanks to everyone for coming here on such short notice. I know things are moving faster than we had thought, and some surprises have come your way." He paused for a minute and they all took a minute to acknowledge their humanoid companions. "And, some things have gone according to plan, while others have definitely not," Ramsey said, looking down the table at Lucas.

He glanced at Kai. "We need to adjust and react quickly sometimes on the fly at bit. We can't always gather and vote on everything that happens. So, for example, sending you your companions was my decision. I felt it was necessary to get acquainted now, in your setting, because we don't have much time, and frankly we're at a risky point; what happened to Kai is proof of that. Before we go deep into all the details, I want to introduce you all to Tim Lucas at the other end of the table."

Lucas slowly nodded. "Call me Lucas, please."

"And his two *companions* are Sky and Lexi. The three of them have been together for almost two years now. So they have quite a head start on the three of you. Maybe they could share a few tips. I will tell you that Lucas has shared a lot with me, and modifications have been made, which have also been incorporated into your companions. So Lucas has been on the front lines here for us for a while now. He and his team were responsible for the recent missions across the mainland U.S., and for the very recent freeing of Kai.

"Now, that situation has exposed us to great risk. We'll get into the details of that soon. Kai's family is still in danger, and I'm focused on that as well. Lucas, did you want to say anything to the group?"

Lucas looked surprised.

"Well, um, maybe? Thanks for putting me on the spot, Ramsey. Nice to meet everyone. Not right now. Let me listen in for a while. This is my first one of these meetings."

"Fair enough. Let's review where we are and where we go from here. As you're all aware the latest is that the border with Harmony has been closed. They, meaning the federal government, have also seized our national parks and public lands. Harmonians can go there, but Hope residents aren't allowed. This is the first time the feds have chosen sides publicly. And, of course, the attacks on peaceful protests was a joint effort between Harmony and the feds. Any questions or comments about that?"

No one spoke. "OK, I'll continue with the 'what's next' part."

"Hold on," Claire said. "Before you outline the plan, I have a fundamental question for you, Ramsey. Why do you need us? And by us, I mean the original Council members. You seem to have a plan already mapped out in your head. You have the resources in terms of money and ..." she paused for a minute, looking around the table, "for lack of a better term 'manpower.'" She gestured at the humanoids, particularly in the direction of Lucas, Sky and Lexi. "Why did you involve us in all of this?"

"I think that's a great question," added Selma. Bill nodded, as did Kai.

"OK, sure. I can outline that now," Ramsey said. "I also want to set the stage for what will happen next."

Bill spoke up. "Yeah, and I think it's fair to say our involvement in this is no longer voluntary. We've committed crimes against the U.S. We can't go back. There is no way back for any of us now. I agree with the others. With all due respect, we need to know why we're here and for you to tell us, not just the next step, but *all* of the details on your plan, so we can be part of that, too."

"Yes, I understand, Bill, and I will," Ramsey said, but knew inside he could not share everything, at least not yet. He felt a little guilty, but he kept his focus on the larger goal of securing a future for the people of Hope, and for that, he needed to keep them engaged. "So, it sounds like everyone is still in, but pending more details. That's good. And let's say I do, indeed, take this fight on without you ... and win. Then what? Who was it for? Sky? Max? The others? Then humanoids have just fought a revolution against humans. Now how would that go over? The thesis of every 21st Century science fiction movie will have just come true.

"And if there are no people behind the movement, then what was the point? Your companions are not designed to take over and create a new fair and just society for a superior race of immortal humanoids. They're here to help man and woman build one for themselves. They don't have the primitive part of the human brain with all its greed and self- preservation, which was developed over millions of years. I know they're all sitting here, but they won't get offended. They don't have consciousness. We still don't know what consciousness is, and if I figure it out then maybe you can call me God, but until then they're machines, built for the use of man and woman kind."

All were quiet, taking it in. Lucas decided to chime in.

"Well stated as usual, Ramsey. And I can tell you all that if you're not able to stop them, the primitive and greedy side of the brains over there," he pointed in the direction of Harmony, "they'll create a new society of superior *humans* for themselves, leaving us to wither and die off."

Lucas' message resonated with Claire. She could see the pain of his imperfection. The growing inferiority he must be feeling as the Harmonians continued to improve gene therapy while his appearance made him stand out like a pariah. No wonder he's an outlaw on the fringes of society. She teared up a little, as did the other humans at the table.

Lucas was not finished. "And they're doing that exact thing right now. So, you can go back and live out the rest of your lives, breed and create the next generation of inferior humans on a doomed path to extinction. Or we can fight to make all humans share the benefits of innovation and all that it brings. A longer life, better health, and the improved lifestyle brought on by the productivity increases of our creations. Or mostly *his* creations," he said with a smile, pointing to Ramsey.

"And I beg to differ with you, Bill, on the point about not going back," Ramsey said. "No one here is saying you can't leave. There are no repercussions if you don't want to stay. I'll just have to trust you, or anyone else, to keep silent. Of course, I might have to take back Sophia, with whom you seem to be getting along rather nicely."

"Fair enough," Bill said. "I don't think anyone is saying they're out."

Bill looked around the table. All were shaking their heads in agreement. That was enough for Ramsey to continue.

"So what's next? What do we do next? I have a plan, but like we just agreed I'm open to suggestions. The high-level approach is to go on the offensive again. They have shut us out and think they're protected behind their walls, but they're not. And they will find out they won't be safe, at least not until we get what we want.

"It's time for me to reveal some additional details about my operation and what I've been preparing for a while now. Thanks to my business as a government contractor, I have the manufacturing knowhow and capacity to build war-fighting drones on both air and ground. Now, I manufacture and send them off to government facilities, where they are tested, scanned and prepared for battle. I wouldn't risk trying to compromise these drones with modifications related to our cause since the changes would likely be discovered once shipped. Ballgame over for me, us.

"What I have been doing, though, is manufacturing a huge group of soldiers for a non-existent contract. The few human workers at my factory aren't aware of this. They don't ask questions because most of the time they are in the dark due to the top-secret classification of the orders. This order is a little different, though. How? Well, just have a look next to you. Your companions. For lack of a better term, we'll call them spies. And of course, they're no ordinary spies. They make James Bond look like a pushover. With their strength, advanced intelligence, sensors, and I can go on and on, it will be very difficult to defeat them.

"There's one more thing they have that I would like to show you. Ladies and gentlemen companions, please go into the other room and remove all of your clothes."

They headed toward the library.

"Is this really necessary?" Claire asked.

"Yeah, do we really need to see this?" Selma added. "You can just tell us about it, Ramsey."

"It's not what you think." Lucas decided to answer for Ramsey. "You're going to want to see this."

Ramsey walked to the doorway and asked the group to come out. Nothing happened.

"Hey!" Bill said with surprise. "What the hell? Something just bumped into me."

"Hi, Bill," came a disembodied voice that Bill immediately recognized as Sophia. This stunned him into silence. Then all the chairs that were formerly occupied by the companions were pulled out and back in again. There was quiet for a moment as they all realized what was happening.

"OK, this is freaky," said Selma as she looked directly at the empty chair next to her. "Ben?"

"Yes, I'm right in front of you, Selma."

Claire and Bill received a similar confirmation. Lucas did not bother as this was old hat to him. He did enjoy the expressions of the others as they tried to take this in.

"This is a little bit frightening," Bill said. "How can you live with and trust someone who can do this? Wow, I really feel inferior now."

"And I have two of them," Lucas said. "Who knows what they're up to behind my back? Or I should say in front of my eyes, I guess."

"OK, friends, please go back in the other room before making yourselves visible again, get dressed and come back to the table," Ramsey said. "We don't need to do ratings on how anatomically correct you all are."

"Now that you've seen what they can do, let's discuss how we use them. First of all, let me tell you all that I have over 200 unique companion models either fully operational or in final production. I've been able to make only a handful here in my lab below, so the vast majority have been created at my factory in Jackson. I've been slowly sending them out into Harmony to wait for their orders. The next attack is going to be right there at my factory. We're going to destroy it."

Ramsey waited for a reaction. He got none.

"Since no one asked why, I will. Why are you blowing up your own factory, Ramsey? Great question, Ramsey! And instead of answering, I'll let the real Ramsey answer."

He sat down. Everyone looked befuddled. Then the giant virtual screen appeared. On it, standing before the group was … Ramsey.

"Hi, team. Just wanted to be a part of this really important meeting, so I thought it was time to join in," said the Ramsey on the screen. "Ramsey, please go to the lab for the rest of the meeting. I think it will help limit their confusion."

That Ramsey headed for the elevator and was soon gone. The Ramsey on the screen was gone, too. Seconds later, he walked into the room. "OK, I'm back here with everyone. Any questions?"

"No, I don't think anyone has any questions," Claire said. "Oh, maybe one. Why did I give up my life, my future, and my family's future to someone who appears to be insane? Yeah, just that question."

"Fair enough. I'll explain what just happened and why I did it," Ramsey said. "I decided to make humanoid replicas of me because of what's to come next. I'm pretty sure they'll figure out who is behind all of this once I send the companions out to do what's required. Someone will talk to my workers at the factory and they'll put two and two together. I've planned this meticulously, but I can't take the chance of getting arrested. If I disappear from the factory, and from here, they'll certainly find out I'm behind this resistance a lot sooner.

"So, there are a few extra of me now. I've decided not to tell anyone how many. If no one has the exact number, they'll never know if they got the last one or not. One Ramsey will live here, but not likely me for very long. I'll also be able to have one show up at the factory from time to time as I do now so I can limit suspicion.

"Now, someone living with a person could tell rather quickly. If I go to lunch, for example, with a colleague that I'm very close with, that's too much of a risk. The close face-to-face nature of the situation would make them suspicious. So I'll delay going to the factory for as long as possible and when I do go, try to avoid people as much as possible. What I just did now was a test. I wanted to see if any of you could tell if it was my replica and not me. I didn't notice anything out of the ordinary from the group. So, does that make sense and could anyone tell it wasn't me?"

"I couldn't tell, Ramsey, and I've spent quite a bit of time with you over the years," Kai said. "Nice work, you fooled me. I didn't have a clue. I'm not exactly all there right now; I'm worried about my family and still mad at you a little so I was probably not as focused as usual, but again, really good job."

"I had no idea, either," Lucas added. The other humans shook their heads in acknowledgement.

"I could tell!" Sky said suddenly.

"Hah, I'll bet you could," Lucas said. "And you too, Lexi, and the rest of you." He pointed to the companions. "Ramsey has this networking thing going on. His humanoid companion models can detect and communicate with each other. I've been assured that it's not a feature for some future attack on us humans so they can replace us. Right, Ramsey?"

"Maybe. Maybe not. Ou humans had better behave or perhaps I'm flipping that switch and they're coming after you," Ramsey said with a wink.

"I don't have the time to go into the details of all that, but it's an extremely useful and effective tool. There is one other thing I want to remind everyone. Of course, The federal government and Harmonians have extremely advanced and powerful weaponry. You saw how they used shockwave technology against the peaceful Hope protesters, and you saw the result. Everyone was immediately neutralized."

"Yeah", said Claire. "It barely missed me. I was in fear for my life. I thought they had killed everyone."

"Right, Claire, but that's one of the less dangerous weapons they have and could use against us. I have direct knowledge of the nanobot program in the U.S. Defense Department. They can unleash swarms of insect-like robots targeting specific people to infect them with something lethal or a paralyzing agent. It's the most dangerous thing out there. They can be used as an airborne biological weapon delivery system. It can target people of a specific race. Very horrible stuff. So enough of trying to scare everyone, but we need to be aware of the dangers. Let's get back to the plan."

For the next two hours they went over the details. Everyone voted in favor of it.

All were all on board. The next act would be happening very quickly.

JACK AND RAMSEY

Jack Ritchie had made his decision: He told Ramsey he would like to meet, probably just over a video call. As he sat at his dining table, he got a notification of an incoming call. It was Ramsey, whose face appeared on the virtual screen.

"Good evening, Jack," said the familiar voice that matched the familiar face. "It's been a long time. I trust you're well?".

Yes, and thanks for getting back to me," Jack said, "I wanted to reach out to you to just to understand the recent visit from Eli. I was just sort of surprised. I guess I'm still confused on the how and the why. Eli did explain that he met you here in town. I wanted to know if that was intentional. Were you trying to get to me for some reason?"

"No, it was a chance meeting. I'm very surprised you asked me that. Why would I have any reason to do that?

"It just seemed strange to me, but I'll take your word for it. So Eli wanted to come to Hope and visit or did you invite him?"

"I was just trying to be cordial. Told him where I lived and gave him my card. He contacted me weeks later and asked to come out. He's a grown up, so I thought he might mention it to you, but of course I wasn't going to ask you if it was all right. Jack, I think of him as almost a nephew. I would do anything for him and never put him in harm's way."

"OK, OK. Sorry for the third degree. I just had to ask. Thanks for looking out for him. To change the subject, how are you getting along with all the problems over there? Do you think you might need to move to Harmony?"

"I'm not impacted by any problems. They're mostly by the border areas. I'm very isolated out here and I have a lot of security. I'm curious. What are your thoughts on all these problems? Do you think closing the border solves anything?"

"For now, I'm not sure if there was any choice. There was violence against us."

"Who do you mean by us?"

"What are you getting at? You know who I mean."

"No, I don't. Enlighten me, please," Ramsey said. "Americans? Harmonians? HAMS perhaps?" Ramsey said taking a jab at Paul Bento's secret society and Jack's association with it. He knew Jack had joined at one point. He wasn't sure if he was still involved.

"What are you trying to say and what the hell is that HAMS reference? I have nothing to do with that," Jack said in a defensive tone. "We've been talking for five minutes and you always want to start something, Ramsey. You're too much."

"Yeah, I'm starting something, all right." Ramsey paused and waited for a reaction. He wondered if he had gone too far and was making Jack suspicious. The uncomfortable pause lasted a few moments before Jack replied.

"What does that mean?" Jack asked.

"I wasn't trying to anger you. I was honestly just trying to get your opinion because it matters to me. That last comment was a joke really only because of your accusation."

"Ramsey, why do I always feel like I'm being interrogated by you in order for you to trap me? I don't get it."

Ramsey held his tongue. He wanted to say, "I want to trap you because you're a rat." All this reminded him how much he really disliked Jack, but Ramsey wanted to end this on a more cordial note.

"Sorry about that. It was not intentional. I just feel for these people over here and what people like you think is very important to their future."

"I think they need to get their act together and we can all get along better," Jack said. Ramsey almost laughed out loud and again bit his tongue. Why did I expect anything else from him? Us and them. Get their act together. What a joke.

"I think you're right. Good speaking with you, Jack. Goodbye," Ramsey said abruptly. Jack was happy to end the unpleasant conversation.

"Good speaking with you again, Ramsey."

That was weird, Jack thought. That guy is still such an ass. He's just a bitter man.

ELI

Only a few weeks after he returned home, Eli was restless again. What could he do to make his life meaningful? The only thing that had made him feel normal was writing and playing his music. Now that he had few prospects on that front, he felt lost again. Hope was still in the back of his mind. It was almost like an odd new frontier. Go backwards to move forward. But the timing was horrible to even consider going back to Hope. The place was falling apart, and the borders had been closed. As he was pondering all of this, his father popped up on a virtual screen.

"Hey, Eli. I wanted you to know I just connected with Ramsey," Jack said. "And I'm glad I did, but just to confirm that we'll really never get along. I honestly don't know how you could spend any time with him. He always seems to have an agenda. Like he's trying to expose me or something. I think it's odd."

Eli was curious.

"What do you mean? What did he say?"

"He asked me what I thought about the situation with Hope. I guess because he lives there. I mean, I get that."

"What *do* you think? I don't really know — only that you think it's dangerous for me to be there."

"I mean, I told him and I'll tell you: They need to get their act together. They're causing their own problems. Why would I allow their problems to endanger my family? I won't and most people I talk to over here will not, either. So what do I think? We're doing the right thing."

"That's easy for you to say," Eli said. His dad's answer had angered him. "Put yourself in their shoes for a minute. How exactly are they supposed to get their act together? I have everything at my disposal, and I can't do that either. How well would I do if I were born to a family in Hope?"

"Why do you compare yourself to them? You should compare yourself to the most successful people here in Harmony, not them. You just haven't chosen a path yet, Eli. It will come. You need to be more positive. Come to work with me. We're on the verge of some exciting breakthroughs."

"I know what you're working on," Eli said. "Let's all live forever in glorious Harmony. Why doesn't anyone care about making their life meaningful? Let's just extend this pointless existence. Let's wall ourselves off from all the problems of the world. Pretend they don't exist."

"You sound like him now. Are you sure he didn't brainwash you?"

"That's like the most insulting thing you've ever said to me, Dad. Thanks. Yeah, I can't think for myself. Any ideas contrary to yours had to be planted there."

"I don't know. It sort of does sound that way. You've never talked like this before."

"Amazing. Oh yeah? What about my goddam musical? You know it's the story of the greatest generation. The people who saved this country and the world from fascism. Now their country is being taken away from their descendants. What did they fight and die for?"

"Stop living in the past, Eli. That was a long time ago and it's barely relevant anymore. You think too much. Just try to enjoy your life more. You're lucky you have a fantastic life. You can't solve all the world's problems."

"Yeah. Sure, Dad, whatever you say." Eli was in tears and lowered his eyes so Jack wouldn't see. "I'll talk to you later."

Eli didn't know if he had ever been angrier at his father. Now he really wanted to go to Hope.

THE BORDER CITIES

The Council members returned to their homes in Hope, ready to assist with the next steps. They planned to amass as many people as possible along the border. This time, though, instead of thousands, they were shooting for tens of thousands. Each of the Council members would assist with the ground efforts, but the bulk of the work would be done via Hope-based social media, video feeds and other online mechanisms. The federal government has been shutting these down, but they quickly returned with a different address or channel. The plan was working. Within days they had thousands at the borders. What they didn't expect was the determination of those who had joined the cause to buckle down for the long term. The protesters were starting to build impressive temporary structures along the wall for them to live 24/7. Because people really had nothing else to do, they had taken to this cause in a big way. Just months ago, there was almost no organized resistance except for Ramsey and his small team. Now, people had awakened. A major turning point had been the shockwave attack on the first group of protestors, which both appalled and motivated them.

As the groups grew, the Council members felt it was safe to join the protest. Selma and Ben walked along the wall outside Miami witnessing the scene first hand. Here, the typical short rainstorms were the biggest problem, so people had done their best to create shelter with tarps and other coverings. They would peel them back when the rain passed. One such rain had just finished, and Selma could feel the hot moisture in the air as it was lifted by the sun. It was June, the likely beginning of a hot summer. The people looked ready for long haul, though. And ready for change. Ben seemed to be taking it all in, and Selma had noticed him changing. He was learning about her, the environment they lived in and the people who inhabited it. One of them was playing, loudly, a song that fit the scene quite profoundly.

Selma knew the song; her parents played it during her childhood. It was a Los Lobos song called "A Matter of Time." Now nearly a century old, it nonetheless seemed to represent the same struggle: people facing a border, a wall, and a dream of escaping poverty. Selma reflected on the irony: How unfair it seemed that the grandchildren and great grandchildren of those who made it to the United States from Mexico and other places south were in the same exact position again. Her thoughts were interrupted by Ben.

"I was wondering about something," he said as they walked slowly along the virtual wall.

"I haven't heard you use that term before: *wondering*. I actually didn't know it was something you even did."

"Well, I've learned how to use the word by our conversations, I guess. I do seek information like you do, but the way I wonder and the way you do is, I'm certain, much different mechanically."

"I don't really care about the mechanics of it. I like it."

"Good. Back to my question, then. What is it like to dream? I know you can dream at night and you can dream about the future. I'm actually wondering about both types of dreams."

Selma looked even more surprised this time before answering.

"You are extremely interesting, you know that, Ben? More interesting than anyone I've ever dated before. I'll tell you what I never dreamed would happen? Having a relationship with someone like you. I would have never thought I would be open to something like that nor did I think it could be meaningful."

"Thank you. So that is dreaming of the future, and it sounds like your dreams have changed since you met me?"

"You have no idea. Come to think of it, my dreams of what my life could be were very limited before. You know, you don't really notice that you're pondering your future as you go about your day. It just happens. All the things that happen to you daily impact these dreams. A promotion, a breakup, or even someone just saying something bad about you."

Ben paused. "I have trouble understanding the concept because I have no childhood to reflect on and no finality to worry about. At some point I know I will no longer exist, but I don't have any idea when that will be or why. I'm also not trying to improve myself or my standard of living like most humans are. I am what I am until I no longer *am*. Does that make sense?"

"Wow, maybe this is too deep for me," Selma replied. "I guess you're right, though. I think my plans or dreams are based a lot on my life so far and how long I have left to capture them."

They continued walking, witnessing the people continuing to arrive and setting up their makeshift home along the divider. In some ways it made Selma feel good, but there was a lingering feeling of dread. How would this turn out for them? For me? She couldn't help but think that success was unlikely. That *they*, the Harmonians, would win. They had all the resources and it always went the way of the people who had the money.

A STRANGER IN UTAH

In Kanab, Utah, a stranger had come to town. He sat in the local diner every morning wearing his Fedora with the brim pointed slightly down covering his eyes most of the time. He was generally well dressed and looked the part of a Harmonian businessman. Except there was little business in Kanab. It hadn't changed much since the days of early American films like 'The Outlaw Josey Wales' were filmed here. The only thing Kanab had these days was a giant power station, recently enhanced and expanded to facilitate the great power needs of the border wall. In past years, an expansion of this sort would bring new life, new jobs to a region. This was no longer the case. The station was staffed almost exclusively by robots and a few humanoids. Only a few senior management staff and a security chief had moved into town to run the station. As a result, Kanab's population had not increased much at all. Being located between Bryce Canyon and Zion National Park, it remained mostly a playground for adventure-seeking Harmonians and some Hope tourists, but the recent events in Hope had halted all visitation from there. The hotels were not as full as they were in recent years and the restaurants weren't either. So the man sat mostly alone every morning.

It took a long time for locals to notice the man because the restaurant was staffed without humans. The humanoids who operated the establishment were not trained to be suspicious of people. Their charter was to please the customer, keep the place orderly, and, of course, keep it profitable. But noticing him and questioning his motives were two different things. Kanab residents concluded he was probably in town to get a break from the more-crowded West Coast cities. After all, this was a beautiful place close to the much-visited Zion and Bryce Canyon National Parks. The man probably owned a home somewhere near Kanab.

Little did the folks of Kanab know of the stranger's sinister intentions. He was one of hundreds who had infiltrated Harmony, led by a small group of people from Hope who despised the wall and everything it stood for.

ELI IN RENO

Eli was now determined to go to Hope. Though the border gates were now closed, Harmonians could still pass through and return; the process would just take much longer. Eli had seen on video feeds the large gatherings of people forming along the border. The Harmonian-based news outlets had portrayed these gatherings as very negative and dangerous. Essentially, the message was that the groups were made up of mostly violent criminals. This barrage of negative news further strengthened the government's position that these people should be kept out of Harmony at all costs. Eli would find out for himself.

The closest border town was Reno, Nevada, so he decided to head there. The border had been drawn at the bottom of the mountain range. The beautiful area surrounding Lake Tahoe was owned almost exclusively by wealthy Californians. Their holdings also included most of the 30 miles east of the lake on the Nevada side, where many Californians had built homes to avoid the high taxes of the Golden State. None of that mattered any longer as state borders were now obsolete. Eli arrived in an hour via an air taxi. He brought his guitar along and a travel bag for a few nights just in case it was needed. He wasn't sure what to expect, but he wanted more from this than just a visit for the day. It took him an hour, though, to get through the gate, mostly because of the stern warnings of the risks on the other side.

As gate closed behind him, Eli immediately got an eerie feeling. When he visited Hope in Red Lodge, he had flown over the wall. He had never been to a border location such as Reno. He felt as if he were being locked out of a safe place and sent into the wild. Eli encountered the crowds as soon as he entered. They had noticed him and he wondered how they would react. If they knew his name and heritage, they would probably not be too fond of him, he thought. His attire matched the occasion, though: old shorts and unbuttoned shirt along with his beat-up bucket hat; the guitar strapped to his back made him more appear like a wandering spirit. Indeed, people's looks quickly turned from suspicion to acceptance; he seemed like one of them. As Eli walked along the wall, nearly everyone looked normal. There were definitely a few rough characters he passed a little faster, but generally the crowd was young and appeared friendly. He had walked about a quarter mile along the wall before a young, blonde-haired woman spoke to him.

"Hey, you any good with that guitar?" she said.

"Yeah, had it for about five years. Better be by now."

"Why don't you come over here and play for us? We're getting kind of bored and it would be fun to sing a few songs." The others in her group of five gave Eli a similar friendly vibe. He would stop for a while. He extended his hand to the woman.

"Hi. I'm Eli."

"Hi Eli. I'm Sage. Nice to meet you. The others, three men and two women, introduced themselves. Eli guessed the group was made up of three couples. "Have a seat, Eli. Do you want a drink?"

"Yeah, sure. What do you have?" Eli asked.

"The real stuff," one of the men replied, chuckling. "whiskey."

"Oh, I can deal with that. Sure, I'll take some. Can I pay you some money? I don't want to be a freeloader."

"No, no, please. Take this," said Sage as she handed him a cup of whiskey.

"So where are you from, Eli?" Sage asked.

Eli paused for a moment. He decided to tell them the truth. But maybe not how wealthy his family was and his famous father. He pointed to the west.

"Over there. San Francisco," he replied.

"Oh. Well, lucky you," said Basil, the man who had told Eli about the whiskey, in a tone that was almost accusatory. Everyone seemed a bit less friendly all of a sudden, which didn't shock Eli, so he quickly tried to distance himself from the Harmonians, whom Hope residents certainly counted as enemies.

"I hate it over there," Eli said. "It's completely fake and I've decided I don't want to be there anymore."

"That's quite ironic," Basil said. "You have a bunch of people lined up here trying desperately to get where you willingly just left."

Another man, Sander, weighed in with a different view.

"We're not desperate to *get in*. The truth is we're just outraged that they're taking everything from us. And we're here because we want to claim it back again. They can't take our country away from us. Just jettison us off like space trash. They're not getting away with it."

"I agree," Eli said. "As this whole thing has unfolded it just started to bother me more and more. It just happened so quickly. I guess the stage was set immediately when the zones were created. That was a terrible idea."

"We can all agree on that," said Sage, eager to change the subject. "OK, how about we hear one of your songs? What type of music do you play?"

"Lots of different things. I play a lot of covers from the 20th Century." Eli said. "And, I have my own music."

"Let's hear one of your songs," Sage suggested, but Sander objected.

"I thought we were going to do some sing along? We wouldn't know any of the words to his songs. Unless you're famous. Do you have any hits?" he asked.

"No, you wouldn't know any of my songs," Eli answered. "If you don't want to hear them, I totally understand."

"I want to hear one. Just one, OK?" Sage said. "Then we can see if Eli would be kind enough to play us some familiar tunes."

The others agreed.

"Got it," Eli said. "I'll play a song from my album, 'The Story of Henry Hopkins.' It's a concept album about a man from The Greatest Generation. Every song is about a period in his life, each one roughly representing a decade. He lived from the early 20th Century until the early 21st Century. I'm going to play a song called 'June 6, 1944.' Henry is about to drop into France on D-Day."

The group seemed to be enjoying the song and were even more impressed when Eli sang the chorus:

> Will I see heaven, from my airplane
> Will I see God, from my airplane
> Gonna jump, right from my airplane
> And I will fly, just like an airplane

Eli finished the song and his new acquaintances sat there looking a bit stunned.

"That was amazing, Eli," Sage said. "Very moving to me. I actually have relatives who fought in World War II, way back when. I think I heard their stories only once or twice. The people who fought in that war and others don't even exist in the memories of anyone who's alive anymore. They're really forgotten until someone like you brings them to life again. Thanks for doing that."

"Wow, dude. Impressive. Tell us about the rest of the songs," Sander said, now much more interested. "I might want to hear some more."

Eli nodded and smiled. He had no idea how well the song would go over, but now that it was clear they really liked it, it made him feel good inside. He hadn't had this feeling in a while and had been almost ready to give up playing. He thought to himself that maybe he'd been playing for the wrong people all along. The shallow, spoiled people in Harmony now disgusted him even more. All the sudden his pride and his confidence were back. It was exhilarating and had occurred after playing just a single song. Eli wanted to stay here forever.

Throughout the evening, Eli played more of his songs, along with many covers. He had a great time — the most fun in as long as he could remember. He decided to crash right there for the night with his new friends. As he tried to sleep, he wondered what tomorrow would be like, and he hoped it would be a lot like today. Even though he was a bit uncomfortable on the hard pavement, the whiskey helped Eli sleep through the night. When he awoke, he was surprised and a little disoriented at first. Sage was standing over him and he recalled where he was. His head was pounding a bit from the alcohol, which he hadn't tried very often. There were other, less toxic, ways to get a buzz nowadays, so consuming alcohol was considered more of a wild splurge. It certainly felt that way.

"Hey, you OK down there, man?" she asked. "You're looking a bit rough." Eli gathered himself and rather than focus on the pain in his head he decided to focus on the good vibes from the prior evening.

"That was fun last night. Yeah, even though I'm struggling a bit now, it was worth it," he said.

"Good. You're young. You'll be over it soon. We're going to cook some breakfast over the fire. Come on over here and help if you want." Eli nodded. He really liked Sage. He also had learned late last night that there were not necessarily three couples in this group, but only the potential for it. Sage was supposed to be paired up with Sander's brother Chase, but that clearly was not happening, so she appeared to be available. He had learned that Sage and Basil were in fact brother and sister. Obviously, their parents thought it would be cute to name both of the children after a spice, but for some reason to Eli it seemed to fit them. Even though he had Marilyn, he wanted to stay here. Marilyn was perfect. He couldn't think of a damn thing wrong with her, but Sage had this free spirit thing about her. No structure. It felt so good to be with people like that.

"Do you need anything? I'll go get some eggs, coffee or whatever you guys need," Eli offered.

"Actually, we do. I'll go with you. There's a store just down the road," said Sage, walking in that direction. Eli followed. On their walk, one thing became abundantly clear to Eli. The crowd was much bigger than yesterday. Gaps between the groups had been filled in, and the width of the newly formed city extended much farther away from the wall. Eli remembered there was a lot of commotion and a constant flow of people all night, but only with the light of day could he tell just how many people had come. It made him wonder. Who is behind all this? Who is sending all these people here? He decided to pose the question to Sage.

"Hey I've been wondering. Do you guys have like a leader or something who is organizing all of this?" he said. "It's crazy how many people keep coming."

"Not really, but ... there is a guy rumored to be behind everything. You might see his face up on signs if you look around."

"Oh. Isn't that a bad idea? Doesn't putting his face up on signs just advertise his identity to the police, and, I guess, military at this point? Won't they just go arrest him?"

"He was already wanted. He's an outlaw. Sort of like Robin Hood, only meaner, and a lot shorter from what I hear."

Eli's heart sank. "What do you mean by shorter?" Then Eli saw one such sign. It was difficult to make out the image, but they were drawing closer.

"He's a dwarf. When you think about it, he symbolically speaks for all the little people in this country," Sage answered, but Eli was paying attention to the face on the sign carried by people walking his way. It was the man he met in Red Lodge: Tim Lucas. Ramsey is the one behind all of this, Eli thought. He felt numb. What should he do now that he knew this? What side was he even on now? He answered his own thought almost immediately. Maybe the side I'm on is where I'm standing right now.

TRI-CENTENNIAL

Bill and Sophia were witnessing firsthand preparations for the giant celebration for America's 300th birthday, which was to take place right in their neighborhood of downtown Philadelphia. As far as they knew the plans were still on despite the protests in Hope and the masses gathering at the border wall. If it did take place, they would have an important role assigned to them by Ramsey. In fact, they had left Red Lodge with another surprise related to their role. They now had a new guest, one they needed to keep hidden until the day of the event. His face hadn't been seen by anyone in a while. After two nights with them, Bill and Sophia were just getting accustomed to having him around. On the third morning, Bill got up, and walked to the kitchen. Sitting there was Hope's best-known humanoid, Joe.

"How are you doing this morning, Joe?"

"I'm doing well as usual, Bill. Thanks for asking." Now Bill was still getting use to the idea that he lived with not one, but two humanoids. When he was alone with Sophia he almost forgot she was one, and there was a sense of normalcy. Seeing Joe and his famous face reminded him that this was definitely a strange existence and that he was outnumbered in his own home. Being a historian made things all the more bizarre. Bill had read the book and seen the film Joe was based on at least 10 times; it was extremely strange to be talking to this famous character. Bill and Sophia sat down at the table with him.

"So, Joe, I haven't asked you this before, and maybe you don't know the answer. How are you different from other humanoids? Do you have some special skill, politically or otherwise?" Bill asked.

"Actually, yes, I do, Bill," Joe said in his normal reassuring tone. "My responses are actually biased. I'm not just analyzing the data and coming up with the most probable outcome and responding accordingly. Yes, I do all of that, but there's another step. I then consider how that response will benefit my contingency, the people of Hope, and I modify the response based on that information. I can give you an example if you like."

"Please do, Joe. This is fascinating."

"OK, sure. Let's say Emily and I are debating the future of GAP payments. I have all the latest data and I calculate what the actual impact will be at certain payment amounts. When the question comes up, I can respond accordingly, but just giving the facts based on the available data is not my function. My job is to justify a higher payment to sway public opinion. So, I have an additional process to project potential outcomes positively or negatively in forming my public opinion. It's kind of like analyzing what's the worst that can happen, for example, if there's a drop in GAP. Then I articulate that as what *will* happen. It's just like what human politicians have done for years and years. Does that make sense?"

"Yeah it does make a lot of sense," Bill said. "I'm not shocked. I have to say, though, you do it very convincingly."

"As does my opponent Emily," Joe said. "Though we've been created by different entities, we have the same approach. I'm just a little better at it." Joe winked at Bill, which fascinated him. Bravado followed up by a very human gesture, and all done very naturally.

"This is all amazing to me, Joe. Let me ask you one more thing: I believe you've only been seen on the video feeds of debates, never physically in person, is that correct?"

"Correct."

Bill asked the question that had been burning inside him since he first saw Joe two days ago. "So, you've never been able to walk around, and never had a physical body? I guess Ramsey built you one, took the original AI manifestation and somehow merged the two?"

"Yes, that's also correct," Joe answered. "Ramsey built the original AI program as well, so it wasn't as complicated as one might imagine. However, I'm not exactly the same now. I'm not connected to the supercomputer which originally housed my program. That is still in Nashville, but my program was shut down there. I'm a new creation of Ramsey with the Joe AI program. Does that make sense?

"Wow, who knew that? He's amazing. Somehow he hid that whole thing."

"Yeah he's amazing. Since he made me, I definitely need to agree with that one," Joe said, winking again. Sophia decided to weigh in as well.

"Yeah, me too. But you're just a little more amazing, Bill,"" Sophia said, showing a tiny gap with her index finger and thumb.

"OK. Thanks, my dear. Loyalty and little white lies. I'll drink to that." Bill raised his coffee cup. They raised theirs as well and took a sip. It was almost silly to Bill that they also drank the coffee, but it did make his time spent with the humanoids more normal. It could be fun to go out with these two for a few Bill thought, but he wished they could feel the effects like he did. Maybe they'll add a feature at some point like a buzzed or drunk mode so they can act like silly humans for a while. Bill amused himself with that image and smiled at them both. They had no idea what he was thinking, and he hoped they didn't ask, as he didn't want to try to explain *this* silly human thought.

WASHINGTON DC

Homeland Security Director Noah Burns stood at the door to the President Johansson's office for the emergency meeting. Noah wasn't sure if she knew they had a suspect; news traveled fast. Emma had someone up on a virtual screen, but she motioned for him to come in, anyway. It was obviously one of her children, and she quickly finished up.

"Did you have some news for me?"

"Yes, we have a suspect in the bombings and the incident in Hawaii," Noah said. "He's an outlaw from Hope. Already wanted for several murders. He's a very strange character. A dwarf, apparently."

"I know already, of course. It's pretty much everywhere. I'm wondering who figured this out first. Was it the Harmonian police, our investigation or what?" the president asked somewhat condescendingly.

"To tell you the truth, we all got it from online monitoring. He's being hailed as some kind of hero in Hope. Apparently, the protestors at the border wall are holding up signs with his image on them."

"Seems too easy, though, doesn't it? Maybe he's just a fall guy and his outing is meant to throw us off? Either way, we need to find him. Any idea where he is yet?"

"No," Noah said. "He doesn't have an address or license to operate a vehicle. He has no accounts or funds."

"How the hell does he have any means to pull this off, then? There's no way. Keep looking for him, but have you checked to see if there's any association between him and Caiden or anyone else from Hope?"

"Yeah, we've been hitting Caiden pretty hard. As much as the law will allow, to be honest."

"I don't want to hear any more about that. Do what you have to do, but keep it to yourself," the president said. She paused for a moment. "Come to think of it, why don't you just let him go? We've held him forever and have nothing. He'll know he's being watched, but he could screw up and lead us somewhere."

"That's not a bad idea. We can try to convince him we have another suspect and he's off the hook. He'll hear that we're on to this Lucas character and maybe he'll try to help him."

"Oh, and do me another favor, please. Get Emily on to totally discredit this Lucas fellow. Make him look like an ugly, dirty, dangerous criminal with the worst photos you can find. I don't want him being a sympathetic figure. And since we shut down Joe, they'll have no way to respond. Run it everywhere constantly."

"Certainly. We'll have that going by the end of the day." Noah got up to leave. The president watched him walk out, but her mind switched to how her own daughter had questioned her about the closing of the wall. Emma couldn't believe she was so sympathetic to those people. We really haven't done a damn thing, she thought. Why is she against me? She hated this job; it's dividing me and my daughter and making me resent my husband. Emma also wondered how bad this situation with Hope was going to get. She felt like the country may be falling apart and it was on her shoulders to put it back together.

I'm no Abe Lincoln, and I never wanted to be. She felt trapped.

CLAIRE

Claire, Max and the other Council members had been tasked with driving up the number of protestors along the wall. Their campaign in Milwaukee had been a great success. Even in areas where no Council members lived, people had latched onto the message through online channels and joined the cause for Hope. Their message seemed to have gained a lot of traction with the younger generation who before this had very little to latch onto. Claire had even managed to convince Mia to not completely freak out about Max staying there with them, though her occasional snide comments made it clear she still didn't approve. After all, her father had abandoned them for a humanoid; Claire couldn't blame Mia.

Claire and Max decided the crowd was large enough for them to blend in, so they decided to go to the wall and were joined by Mia and her boyfriend Travis. Claire was not sure if she liked him, but she didn't dare utter a word. Who was she to talk when she was now dating, essentially, a machine. They all headed to the spot where the attack happened just a few weeks earlier. It was directly in front of the former access point so it would be by far the most crowded. As they neared the scene, Claire noticed many more people than before, and given the number of camps set up, everyone planned to stay awhile. Claire wondered if the federal police would just send another shockwave to uproot them all, but that attack seemed to have sparked even larger protests. Maybe they would have something else in store. Claire feared what that could be, mostly for Mia who was excited about the scene before them.

"Mom, this is really awesome. I've never seen anything like it." Mia said as they approached the wall. "We didn't bring anything to camp with. I want to stay here. Maybe we should try to grab a spot and then someone could go back and get some supplies?"

"We're not moving here, honey," Claire quickly replied. "We're here to support them, but I don't think it's safe to sleep here at night."

"I thought you were committed to this? *Involved* somehow. Isn't that right?"

"Keep your voice down," Claire said in a stage whisper while nudging her daughter. "Jesus."

"It wouldn't be dangerous for us," Max said. Claire gave him a sharp look.

"Keep out of this, please. You're stepping over the line here, Max." They walked in silence for a while. Claire knew her daughter was pouting and chose to ignore it. She'll get over it.

CAIDEN

Caiden Calloway had been in the dark cell in Washington D.C. for weeks. They used some terrorist provision to jail him without charges or any evidence. The federal government had also pretty much disbanded the government of Hope without just cause. Caiden was angry. He had no idea why they blamed him for the insurrection. The endless, almost torturous interrogation sessions had given them nothing. The truth was, he had nothing to give them. He had no idea who had committed the crimes. What all this proved was that Hope never had a government at all. He was a puppet to appease the poor people of Hope while the Harmonians stole their country from right under their noses. He was sorry he had ever gotten involved. As he contemplated his dire fate for the thousandth time, a man approached and unlocked the cell door.

"They have identified the man responsible for the attacks," he said. "You're free to go."

"What? Just like that? Are there any charges pending?"

"No, no charges, no conditions. You've been cleared."

Caiden walked out. He had to ask one more thing.

"So, this was all just a big mistake, and everything I've gone through was a total blunder?"

There was no response. Caiden was certain the man heard, but he clearly was done talking. He gave Caiden his things, then they walked straight to the door, and just like that, Caiden was free.

"Thanks, I guess?"

It was a warm, sunny July day, and Caiden wondered what he would do next. He had no idea what had been happening for the past two months or what his future would hold. He brought up a virtual screen and called for an air taxi. Once inside, he would connect with his wife and hear her voice for the first time since his capture. He couldn't wait.

RAMSEY, LUCAS, AND KAI

After the Council members left Ramsey's, Lucas and Kai remained. Being the two most wanted men in the U.S., they really had no other option. Kai had dropped to second place behind Lucas after the campaign to position him as the leader of the resistance had taken hold. This had been Ramsey's plan all along, and it clearly was working: Crowds along the border wall had increased and signs of their outlaw leader began to emerge. Lucas already was a wanted man, so he didn't mind being the figurehead for this resistance. He knew that if he was ever captured his life was likely over, and the additional weight that these new charges would bring wouldn't change that. He suspected that they would pursue execution, but if he had no freedom, anyway, that would be a welcome result.

The three men had gotten a bit of cabin fever and needed a break from being cooped up inside the home, which was in an abnormally disorderly state. Lucas wanted to ask Ramsey about the artifacts missing from the shelves and walls and now scattered about the floor. Because they couldn't venture off the property, they decided to go down to the babbling brook behind the house. After a bit of small talk, Lucas had a burning question on his mind.

"Hey, Ramsey. Now that I'm the face of a movement I was wondering: Who's the bad guy? Or girl, maybe? Who do we blame for all the problems?"

"Well, we can make one up," Ramsey replied. "But as I've told you before the truth is, there really isn't one. The bad guy is simply, 'the progress of man.' Sometimes that's a good guy, too, so that's where the challenge lies. In many ways I represent the bad guy, but did I have bad intentions? No, I don't think so. I was blinded by my accomplishments. The drive of humanity, my primitive side, strives for success versus others."

"Yeah, but I want to gun him down in the street. Square off at 60 paces. How do you shoot down the progress of man?" Lucas asked.

"You could shoot Jack Ritchie," Kai suggested. "He's probably not much of a gunfighter, though."

"That's not the worst idea I've ever heard," Ramsey said. "No, I'm kidding. But I do kind of hate that son of a bitch right now. He's probably second on the hit list only to *the great* Paul Bento. Seriously, though, the only way to kill the enemy here is to fight for those who have been left behind. Which is exactly what we're doing."

"I agree with Lucas," Kai said. "We need to have someone or something to blame and go after it. I mean our old company might be perfect. We make the HARE Corporation the evil entity that destroyed society."

"That might not be such a bad idea," Ramsey said. "We can demand payment for their actions so it can benefit the people of Hope."

"Not that it matters all that much to me," he added with an ironic chuckle. "I sold all of my stock years ago."

EMILY'S MESSAGE

Paul Bento relayed the message from the president to the team that managed Emily. She was to discredit Tim Lucas as being nothing more than a common criminal. As always, she would be armed with specific examples to back up her position. The message would likely be well received in Harmony; there would be no rebuttal from Joe, now disabled, or even the Hope government, now suspended. Caiden had just been freed from jail and would not have any time to reorganize his administration — not even to craft a response. Who knew if he would even go back to leading the Hope side? The Harmonians, with the backing of the federal government, funneled Emily's propaganda into the now-empty news feeds in Hope. As usual, the Harmonians did not prepare a speech, only the message that was to be relayed. Emily would craft something better than any human. That evening, her face appeared on all the nation's news feeds, and she began her message.

"Good evening, ladies and gentlemen. I've come to you during a difficult time for our country. As most people are aware, we have recently come under attack from some terrorists, and have had to take steps to protect ourselves. We cannot let these terrorists divide us in any way. I'm speaking to all Americans when I say this, not just the residents of Harmony. We need to join together to halt this evil that has infiltrated our great country. Let me start by identifying this common criminal who is responsible for much of this terrorist activity."

She paused and the screen split; one side showed a photo of Tim Lucas.

"If you see this man, please notify authorities immediately and go to a safe location as far away from him as possible. He is responsible for several murders of people from his home location in Hope. He is not a friend to anyone and cannot be trusted by anyone on either side. Recent proclamations of him as a champion for the poor are completely false. This criminal is a champion only for himself and will be apprehended and treated as the common thug and murderer that he is. As always, thank you all for your time; please be vigilant until this man is apprehended."

AMERICA'S BIRTHDAY PARTY

July 4, 2076. America's 300th birthday celebration would be a strange event. Only Harmonians would attend. Paul Bento and Homeland Secretary Noah Burns felt it should go on. Otherwise, *the terrorists win* was their position. President Johansson agreed, despite some reservations. Many people, some even on the Harmony side, felt it should be cancelled. Harmonians who had sided with their government in the feud wanted to show their support, so they were expected to turn out in huge numbers. Downtown Philadelphia had been decorated with tri-centennial banners on every street. The city looked festive.

Ramsey's team was ready. Their planning had been meticulous. Bill had worked with Sophia and Joe to be ready when called. Joe had a really good disguise but could appear as himself at the right time. He needed to be clothed so they couldn't have his invisibility turned on. He was to be in the crowd, just another guest. The team hoped no one would recognize him before they were supposed to. The main celebration would be at 11 a.m., and Joe needed to get close to the stage without attracting any attention. There would also be invisible humanoid helpers in attendance to make sure their plan worked. Bill's home was only four blocks from the stage, so he and Sophia wouldn't have far to go once they left. They needed to be in place 15 minutes beforehand, and it was now 10:30 a.m. Time to leave.

Joe, in his disguise, would walk with Sophia as if they were a couple; Bill would follow. The number of people on the street was abnormally high, and all were headed in the same direction. Many were dressed in tri-centennial garb while waving American flags. Ramsey and team had prepared a plan to ensure Bill and his companions wouldn't stand out, so the three of them also donned festive outfits. The area was closed off to all vehicles, so they were able to use the streets unless an occasional horse and buggy came through. They made it to the Independence Square location of Philadelphia, where the event was to take place in 10 minutes. It was an amazing sight. The entire city was draped with American flags — from tiny ones on wooden sticks placed into the ground in orderly rows to giant flags draped across buildings. Harmonians had come out in very large numbers, perhaps masking the fact that everyone from Hope was excluded. It also troubled Bill that a great many Harmonians apparently supported the recent actions of the government by showing up at this event.

As they continued closer, it was clear Joe would need to push his way in a bit as the crowd thickened about 50 yards from the stage. Bill and Sophia would stay back so they wouldn't be photographed or filmed with Joe. He slowly pushed through the crowd.

"He's doing well," Bill said. "He should make it without too much trouble." Soon they lost sight of him. After a few minutes, the stage activities began. The emcee was John Hancock, there to re-enact the signing of the Declaration of Independence. He spoke into the microphone.

"Welcome, welcome, distinguished gentlemen," he began. "Welcome to this meeting of the Second Continental Congress." Bill knew the history and it appeared all very well done to him. He almost got caught up in the program, but his nervousness returned as the end neared. Then, something happened and he knew it had begun. Security guards near the stage appeared to be fainting. As this was happening, a man climbed onto the stage and grabbed the microphone. It was Joe. He had shed his disguise and by the gasps and wide eyes in the crowd it was clear that most people immediately recognized him. As Joe addressed the crowd, all were stunned into silence.

"Ladies and gentlemen, good afternoon," Joe began. "I've come to address everyone here and those watching across the country. As you are all aware, the United States has been divided into two groups, Hope and Harmony. Since this division was originally positioned as an opportunity to create a brighter future for the less fortunate, we need to take an immediate look at the current results."

President Johansson was watching at home and called Homeland Security Director Noah Burns immediately.

"What is going on?" she said frantically. "How is this happening and why isn't security taking him off the stage?"

"I know. I know. We're trying, Madam President," he said. "Apparently guards all around the stage have been restrained. We're trying to get the other security personnel up there, but due to the large crowd, it's taking some time."

"What about the goddam military? Get him off the stage!" she yelled.

"We are. Stand by."

Joe continued, "So the experiment has failed. And since it has failed, I call for immediate reunification of Hope and Harmony. The human failure to provide oversight to technological advances is to blame, I'm afraid. Specifically, much of the responsibility is on the HARE Corporation, and others like it. They profited to the detriment of humanity to benefit a few individual humans."

An object coming from the sky was hurling in Joe's direction just as he was finishing. "And on America's 300th birthday, most Americans cannot even go to the Grand Canyon or attend the birthday party planned for *all* Americans to celebrate ..."

The object struck Joe in the center of his chest and lodged there. His head and the top of his torso melted as horrified spectators watched. Joe's lifeless legs fell to the ground. People began to run in terror.

The president called the homeland security boss again.

"Oh my God!" she said. "What was that? That's the worst thing I've ever seen in my life!"

"I'm not sure exactly. It's some sort of missile designed to limit shrapnel and kill with heat. It's good for targeting a bad actor and limiting civilian casualties," he said.

"But we just melted the face of Tom Joad in front of the whole world!" the president yelled, closing the popup screen. My political career is finished, she thought. She didn't even want to look at the faces of her husband and daughter Charlotte. She tried to sneak back in the room, and both looked at her with looks of horror on their faces. Her daughter's look turned accusatory.

"Mom, did you do that?" Why did you do that?"

"No. Not really."

"What do you mean, 'not really?' That means you *are* involved. I'm leaving." Charlotte bolted from the room.

At the scene of Joe's assassination, Bill and Sophia stayed put. People were running frantically from the area, often bumping right into them. After a while, Bill looked at Sophia. "I'm trying to remain calm on the outside, but I'm actually freaking out. Does this sort of thing bother you? I know it's a strange question, but I honestly don't know."

"I know it bothered you. I could tell immediately," she replied. "So, if it bothers you, it bothers me."

"Yeah, maybe that's what I guessed. I think it's OK too. Not perfect, but OK. At some point I might change my mind about that depending on the topic. It might be good for us if you disagreed with me sometimes. Not this time, though."

"I can disagree with you. Sometimes you think I'm simple, but I'm not. We're going to evolve in that way." Bill nodded and snapped back into the reality of the situation.

"This is crazy. Let's get out of here," Bill said. "I assume you have the entire episode on video?"

"Yes, I have the whole thing."

"Perfect, although that was horrible, the video will help us enormously," Bill said. "I was just getting to know Joe, and I miss him already. It's like I just lost a new friend."

"Yeah, me, too," Sophia replied.

Bill wondered what that really meant. He wondered if they had some special bond via their communication features or something. He put it out of his mind for now and they went back to his house.

THE WALL

Eli and the others gathered at the wall near Reno witnessed the brutal scene in Philadelphia on a video feed. Everyone had their personal virtual screens up everywhere, but most people were barely watching — and only to mock the proceedings. Suddenly, someone in the crowd had yelled, "That's Joe in Philly!" People turned their attention toward the screens and went silent to hear him. When the missile struck him, there was a period of shock, then anger erupted. The Harmonians had taken the conflict to a new level. If there had been any chance of people tiring of this protest and going home, Harmonians had killed that off when they killed Joe. Within an hour, crowds growing much, much larger. Before the destruction of Joe, protesters arriving in Reno had tricked down to a few per hour. Now, who knew how many would show up. Eli looked at Sage.

"Wow, now they're really coming," he said. "I've never seen so many people before. Is everyone in Hope coming here?"

"I hope so," she said. "No reason to stay home and go back to your lousy life now. They just woke everyone up." People continued to arrive carrying signs of Lucas, but now ones of Joe, too. A humanoid and a dwarf are representing these people, Eli thought. What a strange world we live in. Just then, the crowd was abuzz over a new video feed. It was a replay of the attack on Joe with commentary and annotations. Apparently, someone at the event had recorded the assassination because neither the Harmonians nor the federal government would allow this to be shown. Eli watched, too. Joe's killing looked worse than it had when he saw it live. It was in slow motion, and it obviously had a lot to do with the huge number of people now showing up. The residents of Hope were seeing this repeatedly and were getting angrier.

"That's not even a person being killed," Eli said, "but it seems worse in some ways."

"I know what you mean," Sage said. "It makes them look really evil, like they always intended to separate from us permanently. And that they use all their military might to make sure we never get our country back. They're just mobilizing people on the other side."

"Maybe on both sides. I mean, you know where I'm from. I don't know how everyone feels over there, but I'm sure it turned some people this way."

"I hope so. I really hope so." Sage turned her attention to some people headed her way. One was very familiar and had a guitar on his back, just like Eli. She nudged Eli and pointed out the guitarist. He looked over and immediately recognized the figure.

"Woody Guthrie replica. Pretty cool."

"Yeah, you should play with him. Do you mind if I ask? What do you call the people who brought him —owners?"

"Please, no. That's sounds horrible. I just call them friends. Like ask, 'Hey, do you think your friend would mind playing with my friend?'"

Sage nodded and walked over to the group. They all immediately headed back. Woody was quite impressive. Eli guessed he was a HARE model, but resolved not to identify himself or who his father was. It would be embarrassing at best and dangerous at worst.

"Hey, my friend," said a long-haired bearded man next to Woody. "I understand you're a musician. The lady here asked if you and Woody could play together. What do you say?"

"I'm up for it." Eli walked over and picked up his guitar and pointed to a clearing against the wall. He figured he would introduce himself to Woody as well. "Pleased to meet you. I'm Eli."

"Hi Eli, nice to meet you my friend," Woody replied, extending his hand.

"Hey, what do you say you guys play 'Going Down the Road Feeling Bad'? I think everyone's feeling kind of bad right now so it's probably the right thing to sing just about now," said the long-haired man.

"I know that one; let's do it," Eli said. "And it doesn't have to be just us. You all know the words too. Let's all sing it together so we can let it out. I mean all the bad feelings. Then maybe we'll do a more positive tune."

As they began to play, a crowd gathered. By the time they finished the first song, hundreds of people were watching. Eli and Woody stood on two crates enabling everyone to see. Then they played Woody's most famous tune, "This Land is Your Land." After a few minutes, thousands were joining in. Singing this song here with all these people made Eli smile, and he almost shed a tear. He felt for the first time that his life had a purpose.

HOME IN THE BLACK HILLS

Ramsey, Kai, Lucas and many of the humanoids, including Sky and Lexi, gathered around the main table in Ramsey's home. He had summoned everyone for a quick meeting.

"We need to leave here. Very quickly. I've been discovered, and my factory in Jackson will be exploding within a few minutes to make sure they discover as little as possible about what we were building there. My other home near Durango has been set up as a place for them to look for me. I've sent some signals indicating I'd relocate there. They'll continue to watch and nothing will happen. They'll waste their resources on watching for me there. I have a secret location in the Black Hills that no one knows about where all of us will go next. I've been preparing for this for some time. It's less visible, almost all underground, and we should be safe there while things get heated across the country.

"I'll need everyone to act quickly to take our things from here, especially from down below in the production areas. In addition to the BlueJay, we have other vehicles we can use to make a quick exit. They all know the way. We need to make sure no one is followed, so we'll all take different programmed paths and monitor any vehicles that might be following. Lucas, Kai, Sky, and Lexi, you can leave first with Jay. We need to make sure you get there safely. The other humanoids here will pack the rest of the items and move them over. If any of them are followed they'll peel off and try to lose their pursuers. The good news is that I've already moved quite a bit of things there already. You've probably noticed things missing throughout the house; I've been preparing for us to move and I want my things. They give me comfort, plus I need what's downstairs to keep our movement going."

"Ah so that's what was going on," Kai said. "I didn't think you needed a renovation. How can you improve on perfection?"

"Yeah, I'm going to miss this place. We'll make a new home in another beautiful spot in America."

"Can I go home to Hawaii instead?" Kai said as if joking, but Ramsey could see the pain on his face.

"I'm afraid not, my friend. I'm sorry you and your family are still in limbo. I don't have an answer. At some point we may be able to take them to our new place. I'm not sure if you want that or if they'll be happy there, either."

"I know. It's my doing. I just can't help feeling guilty that they'll still be alone and unprotected."

"It's not your fault. I understand how you feel, though. All of us will do our best to reunite you all at some point. That time is just not now."

IT'S RAMSEY

Homeland Security Director Noah Burns called the president with an urgent message.

"Madam President, I have some news on who is likely supporting the terrorists. We have warfighting drones one their way now to make an arrest. It's bad. He is a well-known, although somewhat reclusive individual you may know — Ian Ramsey. I don't know if you even know him personally. He's very wealthy and unfortunately even has government military contracts. We've already raided his production facilities and have taken over."

"Of course, I know who you're talking about," the president said. "I don't know him personally. He's super rich, right? Among the top 10 in the world?"

"Yeah, and he lives in Hope. We should have put two and two together here sooner. He has the resources to do what he's doing, and he's one of the *only* people who do. The humanoid version of Joe tipped us off. We originally questioned his old HARE partner Jack Ritchie and he mentioned his name. Once we heard the name, it made sense immediately.

"How compromised are we?" the president asked. "I mean, with the military products that his company manufactured. Do we know yet?"

"We're trying to figure that out. I've informed all the generals to take everything out of commission that was manufactured by his company. We'll examine it all carefully. They are really close to his residence in Montana, too. We'll interrogate him and get some answers once he's in custody. He'll wish he was never born."

"OK, keep this quiet. I don't need this getting out right now. It sounds like we should have been able to figure this out sooner. I don't need another public relations nightmare like the Joe thing. My popularity has plunged and I'm wondering what my future holds."

What an odd thing to worry about now, Noah thought.

"Will do, Madam President."

THE CAPTURE

The robotic soldiers descended upon the Ramsey compound in Red Lodge with their human commanders following closely. They surrounded the compound from all sides and slowly closed in. They were able to view Ramsey himself sitting at a table just inside the back glass screen door. He didn't appear to have any guards or any other protection. Still, the soldiers were well armed and cautious as they began to climb the rear deck stairwell. Once they reached the top, more soldiers would break down the front door at the same time. Ramsey heard them when they broke in.

"Come right in, my friends," he said. "I'm right back here. I've been expecting you." Other than aiming their weapons at Ramsey, the soldiers didn't respond or move toward him. They were waiting for someone to arrive. It was Paul Bento, the leader of Harmony. He walked up to Ramsey.

"You moron. Why would you do this? You have everything and can probably live another 100 years or more. Now you're finished. They're not going to give you any life extension treatments in prison. Or, even better, your execution may come very soon if I have anything to do with it."

Paul directed some soldiers to search the house. Some looked for the entry to the lower floor, which they knew existed.

"Nice to meet you again, Paul," Ramsey said. "Always such a pleasure. Shallow as ever, I see. I can't for the life of me understand why someone like you would get into government. Didn't your dad leave you everything you've ever wanted?"

Paul was clearly agitated, as were the other four humans, who appeared to be high-ranking military.

"You're going to give us answers. Right here, right now. It will be very painful for you if you don't."

"OK. Sure. What do you want to know?"

"Your factory and the drones you sold to the military. Are they compromised?"

"I'm not sure what you mean. But I'll give you access to the entire home so you can look around. May I get up and give your soldiers access to the lower level?"

"Is this a trick?"

"No, just let me walk over there and open the hidden elevator."

Paul waived in that direction. Ramsey put his hand on the plate that opened the elevator. The soldiers went in. Ramsey returned to his chair.

"Thank you, I think. Now help him jog his memory a little about the factory," Paul told the soldiers. One grabbed Ramsey around his neck for almost a minute. He didn't really react, which was a bit strange to Paul. So, he's a tough guy? We'll see.

"How did you like that? Don't you see how this is going to go? We can stay here for days if we need to. Many painful days for you. The best option is to tell me what I need to know now. These soldiers have advanced torture capabilities as you're probably aware."

"Let me ask you something, Paul. Are you some great being deserving of immortality? By reading the HAMS literature someone just might come to that conclusion. You had to know that HAMS stuff made me sick. To be honest it might be the main reason we're here today. And I love how you try to justify it all by referencing one of the great scientific minds of all time. The problem with your interpretation is that even though the theory is that superior humans *would probably* branch off he never said they *should*. And my interpretation? Any person who would spearhead that effort is evil. Especially someone, like you, who would even take additional steps to accelerate the dying off of the other branch. I know you want everyone in Hope dead. It's never going to happen," Ramsey said shaking his head. "So how long do you plan to live Paul? Do you think you'll live forever?"

"Much longer than you, fool. You're dead already; it's now only about how painful it will be for you before you go. Now let's get back to the question at hand. Are the war-fighting drones compromised?"

Ramsey didn't answer, posing his query again. "My question is very relevant. I just want to know how long you think you'll live. Another 100, 200 years? Perhaps more?"

The soldiers searching the ground floor had returned. One said to Paul, "Sir, there seems to be some sort of laboratory downstairs, but it looks like it's been destroyed."

"That should be interesting. I want to go down there in a minute to see what he was up to. Let me finish up here. This won't take too long. He's going to break." One of the human military leaders followed the solider to the elevator for a look.

"So, Paul," Ramsey said, "answer my question and I'll tell you everything you want to know."

"OK, fine, I'll humor you this one time. If it doesn't work out then the pain really begins. I actually think I can make it a very long time. At least twice the age you are now. Based on the current technology, I think that's about right, but who knows though? With the way technology is expanding they'll probably figure out how to extend life even more. It's a lot longer than you'll live, you terrorist pig."

"So, maybe 150? Is that in milliseconds?"

Paul's eyes widened in horror. It was a trap. "Ramsey" exploded, killing Paul instantly. The explosion was the first of many that soon leveled the home, killing all humans and destroying all robotic soldiers. Ramsey's home was quiet again except for the sound of the creek gently cascading over the smooth rocks.

THE STRANGERS

The restaurant booth in Kanab where the stranger had sat every day for weeks was now empty. He now had his orders, and stood near the Kanab Power Station, invisible and almost undetectable. At 9 a.m., the human security chief arrived in his red AEV and parked in the lot. As the man headed for the front door, the stranger followed closely. A retina scan opened the door, and the security chief went inside, with the stranger close behind. Ironically, the biggest security flaw in the system was the human security chief himself.

Once inside, the stranger found his way to the main switches that powered the wall. His orders were not just simply to turn them off, but to severely damage them. If someone could just turn the wall back on within minutes, the mission would have been a failure; Ramsey wanted to make sure it would take weeks to restore functionality.

The rest of the companion models dispatched by Ramsey to Harmony were also waiting for orders. All had avoided discovery and were ready to strike —at 1 p.m. in the East and 10 a.m. on the West Coast. Like Kanab, inside each of the other power stations were giant switchboards that contained a switch for each section of the wall. There was also a master switch that turned off all the sections for that region. The orders were to destroy all the switches, the main control board, and create an explosion in the control room.

At precisely 10 a.m., the security chief in Kanab heard a loud noise from the control room. He headed that way when its door blew off, debris filling the corridor. He was 30 feet from the explosion, far enough to be physically unharmed, but he was blown back a bit and stunned by the blast. After regaining his senses, he walked slowly toward the room, and out of the corner of his eye he thought he saw the main door to the facility closing, as if someone had just left. The security chief readied his weapon and hurried outside. Maybe he'd see whoever was responsible for the blast. He looked around. Another hot day in Kanab, but it was quiet and there were no signs of anyone. Confused and dumbfounded, the chief figured he had to call someone.

The scene in Kanab was replicated across Harmony. Fifteen minutes after the coordinated strike, border walls had disappeared across the U.S. The masses who had gathered along the wall on the Hope side immediately began sprinting across into Harmony. Robotic soldiers were everywhere, but taking no action. There likely were no orders for this particular scenario. Were they supposed to fire on millions of people? So, the mass influx of humanity continued.

President Johansson was watching this all unfold from the Oval Office. Secretary of Defense Dwight Howard was with her.

"Madam President? Ma'am?"

She just stood there stunned at what was happening in front of her. She finally turned toward him with a blank look.

"What just happened? How could all the walls come down at once? Is this another attack from Hope? It must be. This doesn't make any sense. I just heard Paul Bento was killed and that Ramsey character who was behind all of this was killed, too. I thought this was over."

"Yeah, I'm as shocked as you. I can order the soldiers to respond," Dwight said.

"I don't know. I honestly don't know what to do with this. Fire on millions of people?"

Then she had another idea. "I think I had better resign. I'm not taking responsibility for that." She had been wanting to say those words for a long time. Now that they had come out, it was a relief. Emma knew her move was virtually treasonous, but she just didn't care anymore. She wasn't going to be the one to deal with all of this.

"That's not a good idea right now," the secretary said. "We need order. How are we supposed to deal with this?"

"You deal with it. I'm leaving." She walked out of the Oval Office, tears of relief streaming down her face. She would find her family get them all out of here as quickly as possible.

"Lord help us all," the secretary of defense said, shaking his head. He could tell there was no talking her out of it, so he called Vice President Charles Hanover, who answered right away.

"I assume you're watching this?" Charles said. "What are we going to do?"

"Yes, I'm watching, but we have a bigger problem."

"Really? What could be bigger than this?"

"For you it's bigger. The president just quit and now you're in charge."

But despite the gravity of the situation, news of the president's abdication wasn't a problem to the vice president. a close confident to Paul Bento, he was eager to assist, and that President Johansson had quit was music to his ears.

"I'll be right there," Charles said. "Do you have a plan?"

"Yes, we have weapons and armies, and we're going to need to use them. Please hurry, I have an idea, but I need someone in charge of the executive branch to review it with me and give the order."

"OK. Who's behind all of this? Do we even know? The president hasn't kept me in the loop. It's really unbelievable." The vice president was now just steps from the Oval Office.

"Yeah, the billionaire Ian Ramsey was behind it. He's dead now. He died in an explosion at his home in Montana. Paul Bento is dead, too. He was there with him. We just got word."

"What? Paul is dead?"

"Yeah. There's a lot happening. We need to get things calmed down," the Secretary said. Charles walked into the Oval Office to take his new seat.

"OK," he said, "I will. They just killed my best friend and I'm never going to forgive that."

"I'll brief you on what my recommended plan is while we also get you sworn in. That way as soon as you're officially the president you can immediately give the order."

VIEW FROM THE BLUEJAY

When the walls came down, Lucas, Sky and Lexi decided to venture out in the BlueJay and witness all this firsthand. The police would be focused on the millions of Gappers invading their protected zone. The trio would ride along where the border wall had been and watch the people crossing, knowing they were partially responsible for this astonishing development. Lucas felt excited, and he sensed that Sky and Lexi did, too. The group headed south along the wall toward the area bordering Jackson Hole near Ramsey's factory. Then they would follow the wall as it pushed eastward and around the Denver area where they knew a huge mass of people had gathered. They could see some people crossing along the way, but few people lived in Central Wyoming, so it was sporadic. As they approached Denver the sight from above was breathtaking. It looked like a dam had burst and thousands of people raced through the opening with the energy of a raging river.

"My God!" Lucas said. "Look at what we've done. This is incredible. It looks like they were all in prison and there's a mass escape." Even Jay sounded excited as he asked Lucas if they could get a closer look.

"I think it's safe to get closer," Lexi said.

"Yeah," Lucas said, "Let's hover close to the ground and see what's happening. I want to see if the soldiers are going to try to stop them. Maybe we'll intervene if they do."

"That is not a good idea," Sky said.

"OK. OK. We probably shouldn't do anything. It will be painful not to, though."

As they drew closer, they could almost see the faces of the men, women, and some children crossing and the looks of exhilaration on their faces. They all sat there in silence as Jay hovered slowly above them. They were now across the missing Harmony border wall into the territory most hadn't been to in years. It was a place Sky and Lexi had never visited. The two humans on board held their collective breaths as the robotic soldiers just stood there, witnessing the scene. They were not acting on the people below or even their vessel crossing over into Harmony. Jay broke the silence.

"That's you down there, you know, Lucas? On that sign over to the left. That's your face," Jay said. They all turned and saw a man running while carrying a large sign. On it was a giant photo of Lucas. Everyone nodded their heads slowly, affirming they had done something special. And for the first time in his life Lucas didn't feel like an outlaw, but something else. Maybe a hero, he thought. That brought on a tear, so he quickly realized that he needed to regain his composure.

"OK, that's enough," he said. "We'd better turn back toward Hope and head for South Dakota.

"yes, sir, Mr. Bolivar," said Jay, referencing the heroic South American figure.

"Shut up, Jay," Lucas said while shaking his head. Jay turned the BlueJay around and began the journey back to their new home in the Black Hills.

WHERE ARE WE GOING NOW?

Claire and Max, closely followed by Mia and her boyfriend, ran across the former Harmony border toward Chicago. There were too many other people running with them to count. None of them really knew where they were going, but all hoped for a better future. After 15 minutes, Claire and the rest were ready for a break. They were in a shopping area in Harmony, which appeared devoid of any people except the newcomers. It was a strange feeling.

"Mom, can we go in any of these stores?" Mia asked. "They look like they've closed all of the sudden." Yet, there were people inside, people who seemed to be hiding from the intruders. Claire directed the group to a high-end coffee shop; they could use some water at least.

"Hello?" Claire said as she knocked. "Is anyone in there?" She could see there were people and likely humanoids inside. No response, however. She knocked harder and still nothing. Other Hope residents who had crossed with them tried to gain entry to other stores with the same results.

"I would open the door and let us in," Claire shouted to whom-ever was inside. "I don't know if this will go to well for you if you don't. We won't hurt anyone; we just want some water." Still no response.

"I can get us in," Max said. "Do you want me to open the door?"

"Do it," Mia said. "They're hiding like cowards in there."

"Open it up," Claire said. Max pried open the door without breaking anything. Before they could enter, a man approached Claire.

"We're closed," he said. Claire thought the face and his very deep voice were familiar. She moved a little closer, and recognized the humanoid version of Johnny Cash.

"Hi, Johnny," she said. "You should be ashamed of yourself. Why are you keeping us out of here? We need some water. Don't you remember you're from a poor rural town that's now part of Hope. That's where you're from."

"I'm not from there, ma'am. I'm not a human, as you know. I do what I'm told, and I was told to keep you out of here. Sorry." He forced the door closed and relocked it.

"Do you want me to reopen the door?" Max asked.

"I don't know," Claire said, shaking her head. "I just don't know what to do. All I know is that this is a very, very strange place and I have no idea what will happen to us. Meaning all of us. Them in there and us outside. Something is deeply wrong with this scene. God help us all."

"Who is your God, and how can he help?" Max asked. "I know where mine is and he's doing all he can." Claire just shrugged at him and didn't respond. He had a point.

LAKE TAHOE

Like all the other protestors across Hope, Eli, Sage and the rest of their group in Reno ran across the border when the walls came down. Their climb was a bit tougher here as it involved hiking straight up the mountains toward the California border. They took a few breaks along the way, but within about five hours they had reached their desired destination —the beautiful lake in the serene setting at the top of the mountain.

"I never get tired of this view," Eli said.

"It's truly amazing," Sage said. "And to think they were trying to take something like this away from us."

They all stood there in amazement yet trying to grasp what the future might hold. Suddenly they all heard a buzzing sound.

"What's that?" Eli said with trepidation.

Suddenly, the sky darkened. It was a strange, unnatural darkness, not like something caused by a cloud. The sound grew louder and the darkness closed in. Could this be the Harmony retaliation for their border crossing? Everyone began to run. Eli and Sage hid in a wooded area. They could hear people screaming but couldn't tell what was happening. Without warning, tiny insects infiltrated their hiding spot and attacked Sage. She fell to the ground instantly. The swarm left without ever touching Eli. Oh my God, he thought, they're swarm bots, targeting the people from Hope. He didn't know the government had this technology. He feared for Sage's safety and went down to check on her. She was out cold, seemingly paralyzed and perhaps dying. Has my government attacked its own citizens again, this time with deadly force?

THE AFTERMATH

Millions of Hope bodies lay in the streets, on sidewalks and in fields across the country. Ben stood there in Miami's South Beach next to Selma, deeply concerned for her safety. He had tried to wake her up without any success. He knew she was still breathing, but he could do nothing about her paralysis. Like the others, Ben, Selma and thousands of others crossed the border when the walls came down. Later he saw the army of tiny attackers that apparently had no intention of attacking him, as none of the insects approached. It was clearly an attack on humans, and some humans specifically, he calculated. Ben also noticed that the swarm did not enter the homes or businesses in Harmony. So he stood there with no idea what to do next. He was a humanoid companion without his human, at least for now. He would wait there watching out for her until she woke up. If she never did, he had no idea what his purpose would be.

At the same time, Max stood over Claire and Mia in downtown Chicago pondering the same questions. Bill and Sophia watched it all happen from Bill's home in Harmony. He heard the commotion outside when the people had crossed over. Bill wondered if he and Sophia were in danger and how he was going to explain that he was actually on their side if they tried to get in. There were screams outside then it all went quiet. Bill and Sophia saw scores of Hope residents lying in the streets. Once they turned on the video feeds, they saw that the same thing had happened across the country. Bill shook his head and looked at Sophia.

"Are they all dead?" Bill asked in a panicked voice. "What do we do now? Is Ramsey dead, too?"

"I don't know," she said. "I'm not sure."

"What have we done?" Bill said.

"What have *I* done?"

The End